THE GUNSMITH

446

Deadville

Books by J.R. Roberts
(Robert J. Randisi)

The Gunsmith series

Lady Gunsmith series

Angel Eyes series

Tracker series

Mountain Jack Pike series

COMING SOON!

The Gunsmith
447 – Boots and Saddles

For more information visit:
www.SpeakingVolumes.us

THE GUNSMITH

446

Deadville

J.R. Roberts

SPEAKING VOLUMES, LLC
NAPLES, FLORIDA
2019

Deadville

ISBN 978-1-64540-028-8

Chapter One

"This meeting of the town council in Wentworth, Nebraska will now come to order."

The speaker was Mayor Tom Simon.

"The first order of business is changing the name of our town," the mayor said.

"Point of order," a man shouted, raising his hand.

"The chair recognizes Kevin Hove, owner of the general store. What's on your mind, Kevin?"

Hove stood up. He was a big man, going thick in the middle as he moved through his fifties.

"This town has been called Wentworth for forty years," he said. "We can't just change the name for no good reason."

"Believe me," Simon said, "we're going to have a reason."

Another hand went up.

"The chair recognizes Jim Murphy, owner of the hardware store. The floor's yours, Jim."

Murphy stood. He was in his forties, tall and whipcord thin.

"Mr. Mayor—" he said.

"Tom," Simon said, "just Tom, remember? 'Mr. Mayor' makes me feel too old."

"Tom," Murphy said, "we all know you're a young man with big plans. That's why you got elected."

"Damn right it is," Simon said.

"So changing the name is the first step to those plans?" another voice called.

"No," Simon said, doing away with the "chair recognizes," business, "changing the name of the town is going to be the last thing I do as part of this plan."

"You keep talkin' about a plan," someone else said. Simon looked for the speaker, and a woman stood up. In her forties, she was attractive, dressed well for the meeting, but usually she wore brightly colored dresses in the saloon she owned. "When do we hear about this plan?"

"That's what this meeting is for, Miss Libby," Simon said. "All I need is a chance to speak."

The council members who were still standing— Murphy, Hove and Miss Libby—all exchanged glances and then sat down.

"Okay," Hove said, "go ahead. Talk."

"Has everyone here heard of Deadwood?" Simon asked. "Dodge City? Tombstone?"

"Of course," Murphy said.

"Do you know why you've heard of them?"

"Because people died there," Miss Libby said. "We don't want people dying here, Tom."

"Not people," Simon said. "Just one person."

2

"And who's that?" someone asked.

"I'll tell you," Simon said. "First I need the cooperation of everyone here."

He looked at the ten members of the town council.

"*Everyone.*"

They all started looking around.

"I sense some of you aren't convinced," Simon said.

"You haven't told us enough to convince us of anything," Graham Andrews said. Like Miss Libby, Andrews owned a saloon in town. For that reason, the tall handsome man in his forties was wearing a black gambler's suit. It was what he always wore. "All we know is you swore that if you were elected, you'd revive this town."

"Somebody has to die," Simon said, "in order to bring our town back to life. I just need everyone to be on board with this idea."

"One person?" Murphy asked.

"One man?" Libby asked.

"Yes," Simon said. "One man."

"How can one man's death bring a town back to life?" Hove asked.

"Well, that all depends on who he is, doesn't it?" Mayor Simon asked.

"So is that what this meetin' is about?" Murphy asked. "To come up with a name?"

3

"No," Simon said, "I have a name in mind. But like I said, I need everybody to be in on this."

"What can we do?" Andrews asked.

"Exactly what I tell you to do," Simon said.

"Tom," Andrews said, "do you expect any one of us to kill someone?"

"No," Simon said, "someone else will do the killing. Someone we all agree on."

The ten people began exchanging glances again.

"Do we have time to think this over?" Hove asked.

"Talk it over?" Libby asked. She was the only woman in the room, but her word carried as much weight as anyone's.

"I'll give you an hour, right here in this room," Simon said. "I'll be back."

Even before he left, the ten people began to talk . . .

***

Mayor Simon came back into the room, which had grown very silent.

"So?" he asked, taking up his position at the head of the table they were all seated at.

"Who's the man?" Libby asked.

"And what are we changing the name of the town to?" Andrews asked.

"I've always thought that Deadwood had a nice ring to it," Simon said. "'Deadwood, the town Wild Bill Hickok died in'."

"We can't steal that," Hove said.

"No," Simon said, "but we're going to be 'Deadville, the town where the Gunsmith died'."

Chapter Two

Three months later . . .

Clint Adams' intention had been to ride through Nebraska fairly quickly. His last time in the area—mainly to
cross the river in Council Bluffs, Iowa—had not been all
that pleasant. But upon arriving in the small town of
Lawson, he met a young lady named Melody Hastings,
and that changed his plans . . .

***

Clint met Melody when he went into the local gun
shop. Lawson was not a large town, and he was curious
about the store. He had ridden past it when he first
arrived, and after putting Eclipse in the livery and regis-
tering in the hotel, he went to take a look.

As he entered, he saw the young woman behind the
counter. She was blonde, pretty, wearing a long apron,
with a smudge of gun oil on her cheek.

"Can I help you?" she asked.

"I just got into town," he said. "Saw your shop and
wanted to take a look."

"Go right ahead," she said. "I hope you don't mind if I keep working."

"Not at all."

She had a gun disassembled on the counter in front of her. As he watched she handled the pieces with both knowledge and dexterity.

"You know what you're doing," he commented.

"My father taught me," she said. "This was his shop."

"Where is he now?"

"He died several years ago. I've been running things since then."

He looked around at the weapons that hung on the wall—pistols and rifles of all sizes and shapes.

"Your inventory is impressive for such a small town," he said.

"Oh, I get business from the surrounding areas, other towns and counties. They know that whatever goes wrong with their weapons, I can fix it. And if they need something new, I can provide it."

"New?"

"Or rebuilt," she said.

"What's your name?" he asked.

"Melody Hastings. And you?"

"My name's Clint Adams."

Her mouth dropped open and her eyes went wide.

"The Gunsmith?"

"That's right."

"And you're impressed with my shop?"

"I am," he said. "And with you. Listen, I just got here and I'm hungry. Can I buy you supper and learn more about . . . your shop?"

"Well, sure!" she said. "I'm pretty hungry, myself. Just let me get cleaned up."

She came around from behind the counter and went into a back room. When she reappeared moments later she was no longer wearing the apron, and the smudge of gun oil was gone from her pretty face.

"Shall we go?" she asked.

"You lead the way," Clint said. "It's your town."

"What are you in the mood for?"

"Steak," he said. "I'm always in the mood for steak."

"Then I know just the right place."

***

She took Clint about two blocks from her store, to a small building that looked to have seen better days. There was a worn sign above the door: AUNT SADIE'S. However, once they entered Clint realized that the owners had spent their money on the inside, not the outside.

The walls and floors looked new, the tables and chairs were matching and expensive. Most of them were occupied, but a white-haired man smiled at Melody and showed them to a back table.

"They do the same kind of business that I do," she explained. "People come from all over to eat here."

"That's a good sign," Clint said.

"Oh, I don't think you'll be disappointed in the food."

She was right. When the waiter brought their dinner it tasted as good as it looked, and smelled. The steak almost filled the plate, and what space remained was taken by onions, potatoes, and carrots. In addition, they were brought mugs of cold beer.

While they ate, Melody told Clint about her mother dying when Melody was a child, and how she and her father took care of each other.

"He was a wonderful gunsmith in his own right, and he made sure I knew all there was to know about guns."

"He sounds like a great father," Clint said.

"Oh, he was." Her eyes teared up, but she forced them away before they could make tracks down her cheeks.

When she asked Clint what he was doing in Lawson he told her, "Just passing through. I'm on my way to meet with some people in a town called Wentworth."

"I've heard of it," she said. "It's about twenty miles from here. But I don't know much else."

"I don't, either."

"Then why go there?"

"A friend of mine asked me to meet him," Clint said.

"And are you in a hurry to get there?" she asked.

"Not in the least."

"Good," she said, "then we have time for pie."

Chapter Three

They had time for more than pie.

Rather than go back to her shop, Melody actually asked if she could go back to Clint's room with him.

"If you're not worried about your reputation," he commented. "Sure."

"I'd like to take a close look at that gun of yours," she said. "Why should that affect my reputation?"

"Well," he said, "we could do that at your shop."

"That's fine," she said. "I'll just make sure the closed sign is on the door."

***

They walked back to the shop, entered, and she left the CLOSED sign in the window.

"Let's go back here," she said.

She led him into her back room, pulled the curtains that hung over the doorway. Then she walked to him and began to undo his gunbelt.

"Wait," he said. "I'll show you the gun."

"It's not the gun I want to see," she told him. "Or am I being too bold?"

"I had the impression you were a bold woman when we first met," Clint admitted.

"Then you're not disappointed?"

"Not at all."

She took both his hands and said, "Come with me."

She led him to the back of the room, where there was a long wooden table. There were some tools on it, but she swept it clean with one move of her arm.

When she turned to face him, he had unbuckled his gunbelt and set it down close by, where he could reach it.

"Careful man," she observed.

"Always."

She wrapped her arms around his neck and brought his face down to her. Her mouth was hot and hungry. Clint put his arms around her, enjoyed the feel of her solid body. This was no frail girl who needed to be handled with delicate hands.

He lifted her up and sat her on the solid table, started to undo her dress. When her full breasts blossomed into view, his pleasure doubled. Her nipples were that lovely pink shade that many blondes had. They were big, and as he licked and bit on them, they got bigger.

She wrapped her hands in his hair as he continued to move from one breast to the other, sucking those luscious nipples. Then she leaned back on her hands and lifted her hips so he could slide her dress completely off. Apparently, while she was at work handling guns, she felt no need for undergarments. She was now completely naked, and he ran his fingers through the bushy blonde patch between her legs. When he found what he was looking for, she started, as if struck by lightning.

"Oh!"

Immediately, she grew wet, so he lowered his face to her and began to lick.

"Oh, my!" she gasped.

She continued to lean on her hands, her head thrown back, her hair hanging down behind her. Then, suddenly, she went down flat on her back and spread her legs even wider for him. He slid his hand beneath her butt and continued to work on her with his mouth until she was gushing on his face and beating her fists on the table.

"Ohgodohgodohgod . . ." she kept gasping, until the waves of pleasure eased off and Clint moved his mouth to kiss his way up to her breasts again.

"Oh yes," she said, cupping his head, "thank you. I needed that."

"My pleasure," he said, "and I mean that."

"Well," she said, "your pleasure is what we're going to concentrate on now."

She slid off the table and said, "You have too many clothes on."

They started with his boots, and when they had been tossed in a corner the rest of his clothes came off quickly. She dropped to her knees and took his hard cock into her hands. She caressed it, and kissed it, until it had grown even harder and longer, and then took it into her mouth.

Her head began to bob back and forth as she sucked him wetly. She leaned down to run his hands up and down her back, reaching down far enough to run his middle finger along the crease between her butt cheeks. Then he simply leaned back against the table to enjoy what she was doing for him.

She released his cock from her mouth, gleaming with her saliva, ran her tongue and lips up one side and down the other, then took it back into her mouth again. When he finally felt like he'd had enough and was about to boil over, he pulled free of her mouth, reached down, slid his hands beneath her arms and lifted her up, again depositing her on the table. She knew what he wanted so she laid on her back on the table the long way, and confident that it would hold them both, he climbed on with her.

He pushed her legs apart with his knees, pressed the head of his cock to her wet pussy lips, and slid right into her with ease.

"Oh, yes, please," she gasped, "may I have some more."

He didn't just give her more, he gave her all he had.

Chapter Four

Clint spent several days getting to know Melody's body better, but eventually he had to leave town.

"Will you be coming back this way?" she asked from the bed in his hotel room. They had decided that her reputation would be able to handle visits to his room.

"I don't know," he said, while getting dressed. "Maybe."

"I know," she said. "You can't make any promises. You're not that kind of man."

He strapped on his gun and then leaned over and kissed her.

"It's been great, Melody. Thanks."

"Thank you," she said. "The men in this town are stuffy and boring. And now I have to go back to talking to them."

"I'd say I'm sorry," he said. "but I'm not."

He put on his hat and left the room.

***

He checked out of the hotel, but told the clerk to give the lady some extra time.

"Oh sure, Mr. Adams," the man said. "All the time she needs. You leavin' town?"

"I am."

"Well, it was nice havin' ya in our hotel."

He went to the livery and saddled Eclipse himself.

"That's some horse," the hostler said. "Ain't seen nothin' like him in this town in—well, ever!"

"Yeah, he's something, all right," Clint said, rubbing the Darley's neck.

He settled up with the man, walked Eclipse outside, mounted up and rode out of town. He decided to take his time covering the twenty miles to the town of Wentworth.

***

Even though he didn't push Eclipse, they covered the twenty miles with ease, riding into town early in the afternoon.

Wentworth was a decent sized town, but there wasn't much activity on the street. But Clint could feel eyes on him as he made his way down the main street.

He thought about hitting a livery stable first, then a hotel, but instead he stopped in front of the first saloon he saw. It was called The Queen's Palace, for some reason.

Grounding Eclipse's reins because he knew the Darley wouldn't go anywhere, he entered the saloon.

It had a large interior, with a long bar and an empty stage in the front, but there didn't seem to be any gambling. Also, there were more men there than on the street.

Clint walked up to the bar, the length of which left plenty of room for him. The other customers in the place eyed him curiously.

"Help ya?" the bartender asked. He was a tall, large man with a head like a block of stone.

"Beer," Clint said, "cold, if that's not a problem."

The man smiled, and it was only his teeth that helped Clint tell the grin from the wrinkles on his face.

"That's our specialty," he said.

He went and got the beer and brought it back. The mug was sweating with the cold.

"So?" the bartender asked, after Clint had taken a few swallows.

"Perfect."

The man laughed.

"That's why it's our specialty."

"This is quite a place," Clint said. "But no gambling?"

"It's coming," the man said. "Soon we'll have music, singin', dancin', and gamblin'."

"Sounds promising," Clint said. "How long until it's all up and running?"

The man shrugged.

"I ain't too sure about that, but then I'm only the bar-tender."

"Well," Clint said, "I guess it's not going to happen while I'm here."

"How long you plan on stayin'?"

"Just long enough to meet up with a friend of mine," he explained.

"Here?"

"In town," Clint said. "I just have to find him."

"Who is he?" the man asked. "Maybe I can help you?"

"His name's Ben Fentington," Clint said. "It's been a few years since I saw him, but I got a telegram asking me to meet him here."

"Fentington," the bartender said, shaking that granite head of his. "Naw, that don't do anythin' for me."

"Well," Clint said, "I'm sure I'll locate him. I'll just finish my beer, get a hotel room, and start looking."

"Try the International Hotel," the bartender said. "It's our biggest and best, even has its own livery stable."

Clint finished the beer and set the mug down.

"Thanks for the tip. What do I owe you?"

"First one's on the house," the man said. "See you around."

"I'll be back," Clint said, and left, all eyes in the room following him.

Chapter Five

Clint found the International Hotel a couple of blocks from the Palace. He left Eclipse out front and entered the lobby. From the way the outside looked, the two-story building had been there for some time, but the lobby interior looked like it had recently been remodeled.

There was nobody in the lobby but the clerk, so he walked to the front desk.

"I need a room."

"Of course, sir," the young clerk said. "Please sign the register."

Clint signed his name, then looked at the other names in the book in the hopes of finding Fentington. The name wasn't there.

"How many other hotels are there in town?" he asked.

"Several," the clerk said, "but I assure you, we're the best."

"I'm sure you are," Clint said. "Where's your stable?"

"Right in the back. I can have your horse—"

"I'll walk him around there myself," Clint said, cutting him off. "Just let me have my key."

"Yessir," the clerk said, handing it over. "You can access the hotel from the livery when you're ready."

"Thanks."

Clint went outside, picked up Eclipse's reins. He determined he could either walk around the block, or down an alley, to get to the back of the hotel. Since it was daylight, he chose the alley.

As he came out the other end he saw the livery stables behind the hotel, the doors wide open. He walked over and peered inside. He could see many of the stalls were occupied, and there was a man in the center working on a horse's hoof.

"Hello," he called.

The man looked up at him.

"I just checked in, they said I could put my horse up here."

The man dropped the horse's hoof to the ground and looked around.

"I'm pretty full—" he started, but when Clint brought Eclipse into view, walking the Darley halfway through the door, the man's face changed completely.

"That's your horse?" he asked.

"This is him."

The man came closer, and Clint could see he was in his fifties, with a slightly bow-legged gate that made him seem shorter than his almost six feet.

"So you don't have room for him?"

"For this horse?" the man asked, still looking but not touching. "I'll make room. No problem."

"I can unsaddle him for you," Clint offered. "Sometimes he's hard to handle."

"Oh, don't worry," the man said, "me an' this fella are gonna get along fine. Whats 'is name?"

"Eclipse."

"Hey Eclipse," the man said, "I'm Dusty. How you doin'?" He finally touched the Darley's neck, stroking it gently. Clint was surprised the horse stood for it.

"See?" Dusty said. "He knows him and me is gonna get along."

"Do you need my name?" Clint asked. "Just so you know whose horse he is?"

"Hmm? Oh, sure, tell me your name."

Clint knew the man might forget his name as soon as he told him—or maybe he would if he was anybody else.

"Clint Adams."

"Right," Dusty said, "Clint . . . wait . . . Adams?"

"That's right."

Dusty turned to face him.

"The Gunsmith?"

"Right."

"And this is your horse."

"I thought we established that already."

"Oh, yes, sir," Dusty said, "yessir, Mr. Adams, we did. I'll take real good care of him. You can count on it."

"Let me just take my rifle and saddlebags . . ." Clint removed them and stepped back. Eclipse stood very still, and so did Dusty.

"Okay, then," Clint said, "I'm in room two-D."

"Two-D," Dusty said. "I'll make a note of it."

"Okay," Clint said. "I'll check back tomorrow and see how you're getting on."

"Any idea how long you'll be stayin'?" Dusty asked.

"No," Clint said, "but at least until tomorrow."

"Right, right."

"Rub him down good," Clint said.

"I'm gonna treat him with kid gloves, Mr. Adams," Dusty said. "You can count on it."

"The clerk said I could get into the hotel from here?"

"Oh sure," Dusty said, "there's a back door right there. Just take the stairs up to your floor."

"Thanks," Clint said.

He stepped from the livery and spotted the back door right away.

Chapter Six

Mayor Tom Simon looked up from his desk as his office door opened and his right-hand man, Rick Croxton, entered.

"What is it?" Simon asked.

"The word's gone out," Croxton said. "The Gunsmith's in town."

"Where?"

"At the International House."

"And?"

"He's lookin' for his friend, Fentington," Croxton said. "What do we do?"

"Let him look," Simon said. "The plan is finally in motion."

***

The room was impressive enough to make Clint wonder why the owners of this hotel had spent all their money on the lobby and rooms, leaving the outside looking so run down? On the other hand, maybe they just hadn't gotten to the outside, yet.

Now that he'd had a drink, taken care of Eclipse and been to his room, it was time to take care of the rumbling in his stomach.

He went back downstairs to the empty lobby, walked to the doorway that led to the hotel diningroom and looked in. It was empty, but for a waiter, who was standing with his hands clasped in front of him.

"Are you open?" Clint asked.

"Oh, yes, sir. Would you like a table?"

"Yes, I would."

"How about one right up front?"

"No," Clint said, "I prefer a table in the back."

"This way, then."

The waiter was a young man, and he walked quickly across the room. He had to wait for Clint to reach him before he pulled the chair out for him.

"Would you like to see our menu?" the waiter asked.

"No," Clint said, "how's your steak?"

"It's excellent, sir. Our cook is very good."

"Then I'll have the steak and everything that comes with it," Clint said.

"Comin' up, sir."

"And can I have a beer?"

"Of course."

The waiter went into the kitchen, leaving Clint completely alone in the diningroom. It was an odd feeling, sitting among all those empty tables and chairs.

When the waiter came back with Clint's beer, he asked the young man, "Why isn't anybody else here?"

"We have a couple of new restaurants in town," the waiter said, "but people will be back. Excuse me, I'll get your steak."

The waiter returned to the kitchen, and then reappeared with Clint's steak dinner with all the trimmings.

"Please, enjoy yourself, sir."

"Thanks."

Clint dug into his steak, determined to polish it off and then apply himself to the task of finding his friend, Ben Fentington.

***

Tom Simon looked up at the council members: Hove, Andrews and Murphy, as they entered the office.

"He's here," Murphy said. "We heard he's here."

"That's right," Simon said, "Clint Adams is here."

"Then we kill 'im?" Hove asked. "Today?"

"Gentlemen," Simon said, "that's not all there is to the story. And we do have to concoct a story, so that when it's told, people will want to come here and see where it happened."

"You mean . . . like the O.K. Corral?" Kevin Hove asked.

"That's right, Kevin," Simon said, "just like the O.K. Corral."

"So what's next?" Jim Murphy asked.

"Next," Simon said, "I talk to Tony Bacon."

"Bad Tony Bacon?" Graham Andrews said. "Is he the one who's going to—"

"He's the next one I'm going to talk to," Simon said. "After that, I'll let you know what we're going to do."

"And what are we supposed to do until then?" Hove asked.

"Go back to work," the mayor said. "All of you."

The three men looked at each other, then nodded and filed out of the office.

Croxton came into the office and closed the door.

"I told them not to bother you," he said. "They wouldn't listen."

"It's all right," Simon said. "Did you find Tony?"

"Yes."

"Why isn't he here?"

"He, uh, says you have to come to him."

Simon stared at Croxton for a few moments, then said, "Yeah, well, that figures." He came around from behind his desk.

"Where are you going?" Croxton asked, as Simon walked past him.

"Where do you think?" Simon asked. "To talk to Bad Tony Bacon."

Chapter Seven

"How was it?" the waiter asked.

"Very good." He'd had better steaks before, but this one had been good enough to enjoy.

"Coffee?"

"Please. And a piece of pie."

"What kind?"

"Anything but rhubarb."

The waiter laughed.

"I know what you mean."

He hurried to the kitchen and returned with a mug of coffee and a piece of apple pie.

"Thanks."

Again, not the best coffee and pie he'd ever had, but he enjoyed them.

***

Tom Simon entered the Saddle & Spur Saloon, spotted Tony Bacon sitting near the back with two other men. They were laughing, and drinking whiskey.

Bacon looked up at Tom Simon as he approached.

"Well, Mr. Mayor," he said. "Slummin'?"

"We need to talk," Simon said.

"So talk," Bacon said, with a shrug.

"Alone."

"You heard the man, boys," Bacon said. "See you later. Go visit our friend, Greg, behind the bar."

"Yeah, sure," one of them said. Both stood up and moved to the bar.

Simon sat down.

"It makes you happy to force me to come here, doesn't it?" Simon asked.

"Why not?" Bacon asked. "We both used to come here, remember? Before you became some high mucky-muck politician."

"That was when we were young," Simon said.

"So why are you here now?"

"Because you wouldn't come to my office."

"Okay," Bacon said, "so what's this all about?"

"The Gunsmith," Simon said. "Does the name ring a bell?"

"A big one," Bacon said, leaning forward. "Tell me more."

***

Clint finished his coffee and pie, thanked the waiter and paid his bill. He stepped into the lobby and then out the front door of the hotel. There were a few people walking on the street, but it still looked like a town that was asleep. He decided to take a walk, check some of the other hotels for his friend Ben "Potatoes" Fentington. They had met over ten years ago when they both served on the same posse. Fentington told Clint he'd been called "Potatoes" since he was a kid, because that was all he would eat.

They became friends by the time the posse disbanded, and stayed in touch over the years. It was only a few weeks ago that a telegram from Potatoes reached Clint, and he headed for Wentworth, Nebraska.

As he walked the streets he recalled that the telegram did not say why Potatoes wanted him to come to Wentworth, just that he was needed. But that was all a friend usually had to say to get Clint Adams to run headlong into someone else's troubles. As much as he swore he would do it less, he was doing it more.

***

He found three more hotels in town, and none of them had Fentington's name on their register. Later in the afternoon, he found himself back at the Queen's Palace saloon.

"Haven't found your friend, yet?" the bartender asked, setting a beer down in front of him.

"Afraid not," Clint said.

He'd noticed there were more men in the saloon, and more people on the street. He also noticed they were eyeing him curiously.

"You must not get many strangers in town," he said to the bartender.

"How's that?"

"Well, people seem to be very interested in me."

"We get our share," the barman said, "but not many like you."

"Like me?"

"You know," the man said, "famous."

"So the word's gone out, has it?"

"Ever since you registered at the hotel," the bartender told him. "Yeah, we sort of keep track of things like that."

"I guess that means I can expect a visit from your local lawman. Who would that be, by the way?"

"We have a town marshal named Mark Ellis."

"Been here long?"

"As a matter of fact, he was hired last month."

"Any experience?"

"He's in his late thirties, and yeah, he had some experience. That's what I heard, anyway. The town council hired him."

"Is he any good?"

"Hard to tell after a month, but he makes his rounds, comes in here every night, checks us out, doesn't have a drink, and moves on. Seems like a real serious sort of fella."

"Maybe I shouldn't wait for him to find me," Clint said. "He might know something about my friend."

"His office is right up the street," the bartender said. "Got his name hangin' over the door."

"He put it there?"

"No, the town council did," the bartender said.

"I don't think he likes it, but . . ." He shrugged.

"What's your name?"

"Cupp," the man said, "Scott Cupp."

"Thanks for talking to me," Clint said. "This time I'll pay for my beer."

"This time I'll charge ya!" Cupp said, with a laugh.

Clint paid for his beer, then turned and headed for the marshal's office.

Chapter Eight

"So you want me to kill the Gunsmith," Tony Bacon said, when Mayor Simon stopped talking.

"That's all you got out of everything I just said?" Simon asked.

"That's the important part," Bacon said.

"No," Simon said, "the important part is that we have to build a legend."

"And then I kill the Gunsmith."

"Yes."

"Okay."

"And you'll need help."

"Will I?"

"Probably," Simon said.

"I think I can take him alone."

"That may be," Simon said, "but it's a better story if there are some others who, uh . . ."

". . . get killed?"

"Just for the sake of the story," Simon said.

"I get it," Bacon said. "I send some other guys against him, he guns them, and then I gun him."

"Now you're thinking about the story," Simon said.

"So when do you want this done?"

"Not too soon," Simon answered. "Let's give time for the word to get out that the Gunsmith's in town. There may be some others who want to try him before you get to it."

"I don't want anybody to kill him before I get around to it," Bacon said.

"Do you think there's anybody in this town that can do it?" Simon asked.

"No," Bacon said, "but that don't mean somebody won't shoot 'im in the back."

Simon frowned at that.

"That wouldn't be the story you want, would it?" Bacon asked.

"Not at all," Simon said.

"Then maybe you oughta think about movin' your timetable up."

"I'll let you know, Tony," Simon said, standing. "Meanwhile, tell all of your cronies to stay away from him until you give the word."

"Don't worry," Bacon said. "None of my boys will make a move without my say so."

"Good, that's good," Simon said.

"Thanks for comin' by, Mr. Mayor," Bacon said.

Simon looked around the little saloon and said, "Do me a favor and don't make me do it again."

"Next time," Bacon said, "I'll come to you."

"That'll work," Simon commented, and left.

***

When Clint entered the marshal's office the man be-hind the desk looked up at him.

"Lemme guess," he said. "Clint Adams, right?"

"That's right."

The man sat back in his chair and spread his arms, displaying the marshal's badge on his shirt.

"You saved me the trouble of comin' to look for you."

"That was my intention," Clint said.

"So what brings you to Wentworth, Mr. Gunsmith?"

"Adams will do," Clint said.

"Sorry," the lawman said. "No offense."

"I'm looking for a friend of mine," Clint said. "He sent me a telegram saying he was here in your town, and needed my help."

"That a fact?" Marshal Ellis asked. "What's his name?"

"Fentington," Clint said, "Ben Fentington. His friends call him 'Potatoes'."

"Potatoes?" Ellis laughed. "I never heard of anybody usin' that name. What's he look like?"

"Big, lumpy guy," Clint said. "Lumpy" was actually the only way to describe Fentington.

"Well," Ellis said, "we had some strangers in town—when did you hear from him?"

"About three weeks ago," Clint said.

"Yeah, we've had strangers in the last three weeks, but," he started shaking his head, "that description of your friend doesn't strike a chord with me."

"I checked all the hotels," Clint said. "Are there any rooming houses in town?"

"Several," Marshal Ellis said. "I'll tell you where they are."

"Thanks, I appreciate it."

Clint listened attentively for the next few minutes, committing it all to memory.

"I wish you luck," the marshal finished.

"Thanks." Clint headed for the door.

"One more thing," Ellis said.

"Yeah?"

"We've got a few hotheads in town," the lawman said. "Maybe you could avoid killin' any of them?"

"Hey," Clint said, "if they leave me alone, I'll leave them alone."

Chapter Nine

The first rooming house he checked was run by a handsome woman named Martha Folsom. She looked to be in her well-preserved forties.

"I'm sorry, sir," she said, standing in the doorway of her house, "but that name—Fentington?—doesn't bring anyone to mind."

"How many boarders do you have at a time?" he asked.

"I can fit a dozen in here," she said, waving an arm at her two-story house, "but usually I top out at seven or eight at a time."

"And nobody else takes in your boarders?"

"I talk to everyone before I let them in," she said, folding her arms. "You interested?"

"I have a hotel room."

"I can give you a better rate," she said, "and better food. Plus, maybe some fringe benefits."

"Fringe benefits?"

She smiled, making her pretty face prettier.

"It's not often I get boarders like you, Mr. Adams."

"You know who I am."

"Everybody in town knows who you are," she said. "That's why you'd be much safer here than in a hotel. I won't pass the word."

"I'll keep it in mind, Miss Folsom."

"Mrs." she said, "but you can call me Martha."

"Well, thanks, Martha," Clint sad. "I'll stay in touch."

***

It wasn't a good thing that everyone in town knew Clint Adams was there. But now it bothered him that the street was so deserted when he rode in. Did that mean people knew he was coming? And if so, how? Had Potatoes let the word out? And where was he?

He put the questions aside for as long as it took to check the other two boarding houses, but then they came flooding back. And he needed the answers.

***

"What are you doing here?" Tom Simon asked Marshal Mark Ellis as the man walked into his office.

"Relax," Ellis said. "It makes sense for the town marshal to come and see the mayor, doesn't it?"

Simon sat back in his chair.

"About what?"

"Adams came to see me."

"Why?"

"He's lookin' for his friend."

"Okay," Simon said. "We expected that. What did you tell him?"

"That I never heard of him."

"Did he accept that?"

"He did," Ellis said, "but he's checking all the hotels and boarding houses."

"That doesn't matter," Simon said. "He's not going to find anything."

"There's one thing I noticed," Ellis said, "and if I noticed it, I bet he did, too."

"What's that?"

"The street," Ellis said, "it was pretty empty when he rode in."

Simon frowned.

"Yeah, I noticed that, too. People were afraid the shooting was going to start as soon as he rode in."

"Right," Ellis said. "That's a giveaway that we knew he was comin'."

"You think he's that smart?" Simon asked. "He's just a gunman."

"It would take more than a gun to keep him alive all these years," Ellis said.

"You're probably right," Simon said. "So what do you think we should do?"

"Move the timin'," Ellis said.

"We can't," Simon said. "We need to build the story-line."

"Then we'll need to give him a good reason why the streets are so empty."

"And do you have one?"

Ellis sat down across from the mayor.

"I just might," he said.

Chapter Ten

Ben Fentington was nowhere to be found.

In fact, it seemed nobody in town had even heard of him.

Had Ben's name been used just to get him here? And if so, why? Nobody had taken a shot at him yet.

He went back to the Queen's Palace saloon, got a beer from the bartender, Scott, and took it to a back table. Once again, he was the object of everyone's curious scrutiny, but he decided not to let that bother him. Not unless somebody actually approached him.

It was after dark, and while there was no gambling going on, there were girls in brightly colored dresses working the floor. One of them, a redhead, came over as the level on his beer mug went down and asked if he wanted another. He gladly accepted.

When she returned he asked, "What's your name?"

"Fiona," she answered, as she set the fresh beer down.

"Can you sit for a while?"

"Well, of course, honey," she said. "That's my job." She sat across from him. She was a slender girl with small but beautiful breasts, and skin as smooth looking as silk. "What's on your mind, honey?" she asked. "You look . . . lost."

"Not lost," Clint said. "Confused."

"About what?"

"I came here because a friend asked me to," he said. "But I can't find him, and nobody seems to have ever seen him. And when I rode into town, the street was oddly empty. Do you have any idea why?"

"Sorry, honey," she said, "I sleep through most of the morning and afternoon. If you say the street was empty, I have to take your word for it."

"Okay," he said. "Thanks for talking to me."

"Are we done?"

"I guess so," he said. "I just . . . have to think, make some decisions."

"Like what?" she asked. "Maybe if you talk about it, it'll come easier."

"I'm just wondering . . . should I leave town, or should I stay and keep looking for him?"

"Why would you leave without finding him?" she asked.

"I just have the feeling I've been brought here for another reason."

"Like what?"

"I don't know."

"Don't you want to find out?"

"To tell you the truth," he said, "I'm not sure."

"Where are you staying?" she asked.

"The International," he said. "Why?"

"Because you need somebody to talk to," she said. "I'll come to your room after work, later tonight."

"Look, Fiona—"

"I just want to help you," she said. "I think you need a friend in town."

He studied her for a few moments, then said, "You might be right. I'll see you later."

She left the table. He picked up his fresh beer and carried it to the bar.

"Everythin' okay?" Scott Cupp asked.

"Yeah," Clint said, "yeah . . . I was just wondering about that girl, Fiona."

"What about her?"

"Is she always so . . . friendly?"

Cupp leaned his elbows on the bar. The men to either side of Clint had moved to give him room.

"It's her job to be friendly," the bartender pointed out.

"Yeah, but here, right? At work?"

"Fiona's a friendly girl wherever she is," Cupp said.

Clint drank down half of his second beer and set the mug down. He figured it was time to go to his hotel and get some sleep, get a fresh start in the morning.

***

He almost forgot that Fiona had said she'd be coming over after work. He was sitting on the bed reading when there was a knock on the door. His boots were off, so he padded to the door in his socks, his gun held in his right hand.

"Who is it?"

"Fiona," she said.

He opened the door a crack, studied her for a moment, then opened it all the way.

"It's kind of late," he said.

"The saloon closed late," she said. "But you're awake. Can I come in?"

"Sure."

He allowed her to move past him, then took a look both ways in the hall before closing the door. As he turned she looked at the gun in his hand.

"Sorry," he said, "but it's a necessity."

"I can imagine," she said. "I mean, with your reputation and all."

"Then you know who I am," he said. "I guess it's true, everybody knows I'm here."

"That's this town for you," she said. "The word always gets around when something big happens. And the Gunsmith coming to Wentworth? Well, that's big!"

Chapter Eleven

She was still wearing the green dress she'd had on at the saloon, but with a shawl over her bare, smooth shoulders. Now she took the shawl off and tossed it aside, then sat at the foot of the bed.

"Looks like you haven't been sitting here worried about your decision," she said, picking up the book on the bed. "You like Mark Twain?"

"Like him, and know him," Clint said. "We're friends."

"Really?" She looked impressed, put the book back down on the bed. "That's amazing."

He walked to the bedpost where his holster was hanging and slid the gun home.

"Have you read him?" he asked.

"Just a few things," she said. "I like that jumping frog thing."

Mentioning "the Jumping Frog of Calaveras County" was a good way to show that she actually did know what she was talking about.

"I don't think I've ever met a saloon girl who reads," he said.

"That makes us even," she said, "because I've never met a gunfighter who reads."

He didn't argue the word "gunfighter" with her. He deserved the comment.

He sat down at the foot of the bed next to her.

"You know," he said, "you didn't really need to come up here to talk with me."

She put her hand on his leg.

"And what makes you think I really came here to talk?" she asked in a husky tone.

She leaned over to kiss him, and the kiss went on for a long time.

"Well," he said, when they broke, "if your job is being friendly, you're doing a really good job."

"Oh," she said, "I'm just getting started."

She kissed him again, and slid her hand inside his shirt to run her palm over his bare chest. He unbuttoned the shirt in order to get it out of the way, tossed it aside so that it landed on top of her shawl.

Next, he reached behind her to undo her dress, and the top fell away from peach-sized, firm breasts with dusky nipples. He returned the favor as the kiss went on and rubbed her nipples with the palms of his hand.

She moaned into his mouth in appreciation, then moved her lips to his cheek, his neck and then his chest. He, in turn, pushed her down on the bed so he could remove her dress completely, then began to explore her body with his mouth and hands.

When he reached the apex of her legs and nestled his face there, she gasped and reached for his head, holding it tightly. He worked her with his lips and tongue until she was very wet, then stood and took off all his clothes. As he started to join her on the bed, she put her hands on his chest and pushed him away.

"No," she said, "not here. There." She pointed.

He looked in the direction she was pointing and saw only a bare wall.

"Where?" he asked.

"There." She pointed, again at the wall.

"Against the wall?"

"Yes," she said, "please."

She quickly scrambled off the bed and then jumped up into his arms, wrapping her legs around his waist. Carrying her that way he walked to the wall and pressed her back to it. Then he hitched her up just high enough so that his penis pressed against her wet pussy, and slid in.

"Oh yeah," she said, "that's it."

He started slamming into her, hoping he wasn't going to end up slamming her head against the wall with each thrust. As it turned out, she had obviously done this before. She managed to bounce up and down on him without once hitting her head, although her back did keep banging into the wall. For a moment, he wondered what the people in the next room were going to think, but then he put his mind—and body—to the task at hand and proceeded to pound away, seeking his own release.

She gasped and cried out several times and he could feel her juices gushing and running down his legs, until finally he felt his own release come rumbling up through his legs, his thighs trembling while he fought the release, but finally exploded into her . . .

***

"Oh dear," she said, moments later.

They were on the bed, Clint having staggered over there once he had emptied himself. They tumbled onto the bed together and lay there, gathering their breath.

"You said it," he replied.

"You know," she said, pointing to the other side of the room, "now I'm thinking . . . that wall!"

Chapter Twelve

After they had christened the other wall, they once again lay side-by-side in bed.

"Do you, uh, ever use the bed?" Clint asked.

"We can do that," she told him. "But let's talk."

"What do you want to talk about?" he asked.

"You," she said. "You're a fascinating man. I want to hear how your mind is working this problem out."

"Which problem is that?"

"Why, finding your friend—what was it—Fentlestone?"

"Fentington," Clint said.

"Right. Are you going to stay and keep looking for him?" she asked.

"I think so," Clint said. "I can't just assume he was never here. And if he was here, and isn't now, I want to find out why."

"Do you think something's happened to him."

"It's possible," Clint said. "If it has, somebody's going to pay for it."

"Well," she said, sliding her hand down over her belly to his cock, "I'm glad you're going to stay a little longer." She closed her hand over him, and he grew hard in her grasp. "Now we can use the bed . . ."

***

They used the bed and another wall before they fell asleep. When he woke the next morning early for breakfast, he remembered what she said about sleeping 'til afternoon, so he left her in his hotel bed.

This time when he went to the diningroom it wasn't empty. There were several tables occupied, he assumed by other guests.

"Good mornin', sir," the waiter greeted. "Same table?"

"Yes, please."

The young man led him to the same table he'd had the day before.

"Sir?"

"Ham-and-eggs today," Clint said. "Coffee, black and strong."

"Biscuits?"

"Yes, please."

"Comin' up."

"Tell me," Clint said, "are these people guests of the hotel?"

"Yes, sir," the waiter said, "but there'll be others comin' in from outside. We do most of our business for breakfast."

"Okay, thanks."

"Be right back with your coffee."

Even before the waiter returned with his coffee, more people had entered and sat.

"See?" the waiter said, as he set the coffee down. "Here they come."

"What's your name?"

"Jim Linwood," the waiter said. "Folks around here call me Seamus."

"Okay, Seamus," Clint said. "Thanks."

Clint watched the people filing into the place while he waited for his breakfast, and wondered where they had all been yesterday?

***

Tom Simon looked up from the papers on his desk as Rick Croxton entered.

"How's it going?" he asked.

"People are back on the street," Croxton said, "and they're going into the diningroom at the International for breakfast. Adams is there."

"Good. I hope they're not staring at him."

"We can't control that, Mr. Mayor."

"No, we can't," Simon said. "But we'll do what we can to make this work."

"Yes, sir," Croxton said.

"Okay, that's all, Rick."

"Yes, sir."

Croxton left. Simon wanted to talk to the editor of the town newspaper, *The Wentworth Watch*, but he didn't want to do it through Croxton. He was going to walk over to the newspaper office himself in a little while.

The paper had to be ready to print the story.

***

The breakfast was better than the supper had been the night before. The eggs were perfectly done, and the biscuits were light as a feather. The ham was a thick ham steak. And the coffee was good and strong.

"Everythin' okay?" Seamus asked.

"Perfect," Clint said. "just the way I like it."

"I told the cook who you were, so he'd be extra careful," Seamus said.

"Well, tell 'im he did a fine job," Clint said.

He paid his bill and started to leave the diningroom. He noticed as he did that people seemed to be making an effort not to watch him.

Very odd.

Chapter Thirteen

The editor and publisher of *The Wentworth Watch* was a man named Brian Berriman. He had started the paper ten years before, and wasn't happy about the mayor's plans to change the name of the town. No more Wentworth, no more Watch.

He looked up from his printing press as the door opened and Tom Simon walked in. He turned the press off, wiped his hands on a rag.

"Tom," he said.

"Brian."

They were the same age, late thirties, had grown up together, with Tony Bacon.

"I suppose you know Adams is in town?" Simon asked.

"Everybody knows."

"Well, the plan's in motion."

"Tony agreed?"

Simon nodded.

"This is crazy, Tom."

"This town has to be saved, Brian."

"Why does that include a change of name?" Berriman asked.

"Everything has to change, Brian."

"But the Watch?" Berriman asked. "This can't be the Deadville Watch."

"You'll come up with another name," Simon said. "This is going to work for all of us, Brian."

"You know, when the three of us were kids, I never woulda thought we'd be doing something like this."

"Tony was always the wild one," Simon said. "Even his mother called him 'Bad Tony,' remember?"

"I remember."

"Just be ready with that story, Brian," Simon said. "It'll get picked up by papers all across the country. Mark my words."

Simon left and Berriman walked over to his desk and sat down heavily.

He knew how "bad" Tony was, but to him, with this plan, it seemed like Mayor Tom Simon was the crazy one.

Or was he crazy for going along with it?

***

Clint had enjoyed the night with Fiona, but he was still curious why she wanted him to talk so much. Had she been sent to get him to talk? And if so, by who?

And who else was there in this town for him to talk to other than her?

Of course, who do you talk to in a strange town? Bartenders.

So far he had spent time with only one barkeep, Scott Cupp from the Queen's Palace. But there were others, and now that he had checked all the hotels and rooming houses, it was time Clint checked in at the other saloons.

***

He started with the White Buffalo Saloon, a grandiose name for a rundown little waterhole. There were only a few customers, and a bored looking bartender who perked up a bit when he entered. Probably wasn't used to seeing new customers.

"Help ya, friend?" the tall, cadaverously thin man asked.

"Beer."

"Comin' up."

The man drew the beer and set it down in front of him.

"Do you know a man named Ben Fentington?"

"Fentington," the man repeated. "No, I don't think so. You lookin' for him?"

"I am."

"No offense," the bartender said, "but to kill 'im?"

"Why would I want to do that?"

"You're the Gunsmith, right?"

"That's right."

"We heard you was in town," the man said, "and now you say you're lookin' for a guy—"

"He's a friend of mine," Clint said. "I think he's in trouble. I want to help him."

"Ah," the bartender said. "Okay, well, no, I don't know 'im. What's he look like?"

"He's average height," Clint said, "kind of . . . lumpy all over. He looks like his clothes never fit."

The bartender frowned and thought, then shook his head.

"Can't say I've ever seen anybody like that."

"Okay." Clint sipped the beer, put it down. "Thanks."

"Ain't gonna finish the beer?"

Clint tossed two bits on the bar.

"It's warm," he said, and walked out.

***

The next saloon was called The Lucky Seven. It was larger than the White Buffalo, smaller than the Queen's Palace.

"With the name of this place," Clint said to the bartender over his beer, "I thought there'd be gambling."

"Oh, there will be," the bartender said. "Big things are gonna be happenin' in this town."

"When's that?"

"Soon," the man said. "The mayor said there's gonna be big changes. That's how he got elected."

The bartender was young, and eager to talk. Maybe now Clint could find out something.

"Really?" Clint said. "Tell me about this mayor?"

Chapter Fourteen

"He grew up here," the bartender said, "and decided a long time ago he was gonna be mayor—and change things."

"So what's his plan?"

"I dunno," he said. "I ain't on the town council. Only they know the details. Everybody in town just knows it's gonna happen."

"What's your name?"

"Bobby Streeter," the barman said. "Folks around here call me Muskrat."

Another man with a nickname.

"Okay, Muskrat," Clint said, tossing two bits onto the bar. "Thanks for the beer."

"Hey," the bartender called as he started out.

"What?"

"Don't you wanna know why they call me Muskrat?"

"No."

"Most people do."

Clint turned.

"I'm not most people."

***

The last saloon was one called the Saddle & Spur. It was in a part of town that needed a broom. Clint wondered if the mayor's plans included some cleaning up.

He approached the bar under the scrutiny of the few customers seated at tables, and one at the bar.

"Whataya want?" the bartender asked.

"A beer."

"Yeah."

When the bartender set the beer down, some of it spilled out on the bar.

"Nice."

"Most of it's still in the glass," the barman said.

"What's your name?"

"Who's askin'?" The man looked like he had a sour stomach. It might have been the fact that he was stuck behind the bar of a crummy saloon.

"My name's Clint Adams."

That straightened the bartender up.

"So it's true," he said. "You are in town."

"I'm in town. Now what's your name?"

"Goode," the barman sad, "Greg Goode."

"No nickname?"

"What?"

"Never mind. I'm looking for a man named Ben Fentington. Sometimes he goes by the name Potatoes."

"What? Never heard of him."

"Kind of a lumpy looking guy?"

"Lumpy?" Goode frowned.

Clint looked down at the beer in a dirty glass, tossed a nickel up on the bar.

"Thanks for your time."

"Hey," Goode called.

Clint turned.

"You want your change?"

***

As Clint left the saloon, Tony Bacon stood up from his table and walked to the bar.

"Jesus," Greg Goode said, "that was him."

"That was him."

"You coulda killed 'im."

"I could've," Bacon said. "But that wasn't the plan."

"My hands are shakin'," Goode said.

"That why you spilled his beer?"

"Well, yeah."

Bad Tony Bacon leaned on the bar and looked at the batwing doors.

"He didn't look like much. Did he?" he asked.

"He looked bad enough to me," Goode said.

"Get me a beer, Greg."

"Sure thing."

"In a clean glass."

***

Clint went right from the Saddle & Spur to the Queen's Palace, where he felt more welcome. The customers there—much like in the hotel diningroom—seemed to be doing their best not to look at him.

"Beer?" Scott Cupp asked.

"Yeah, thanks."

It came in a clean glass, and without being spilled. It was the little things . . .

"What's been goin' on?" Cupp asked.

"What do you know about the mayor?" Clint asked.

"Tom Simon? I know I didn't vote for him."

"Why not?"

"He talked too fast."

"You didn't understand him?"

"No," Cupp said, "I just don't like people who talk too fast."

"Tell me about him."

Chapter Fifteen

"Mayor Tom Simon is only in his late thirties, but he convinced everyone to vote for him, said he was going to make big changes for the benefit the town."

"So he was voted in over the incumbent."

"Huh?"

"The old mayor."

"Oh, right, yeah, he beat the guy who was running for reelection."

"And who was that?"

"Mayor—uh, Roger Stewart."

"Is he still in town?"

"Yeah," Cupp said, "he's got a house on the north end."

"I should talk to him, then," Clint said.

"Good luck," Cupp said.

"What do you mean?"

"Since he lost the election he never comes into town, hardly ever leaves his house."

"You don't think he'd talk to me?"

"That depends."

"On what?"

"On what you tell him you wanna do to Tom Simon."

Deadville

***

Clint made his way to the former mayor's house. It was one of a flurry of two-story structures with fences, gates and porches, all in perfect order. He walked up to the front door and knocked.

The door was opened by a dour looking man wearing a royal blue bathrobe, his steel grey hair sticking up in all directions.

"Mayor Roger Stewart?"

"Former mayor," the man said, "thanks to the glib-tongued bastard who now has the job. And what can I do for you?"

Clint could smell whiskey on his breath. Maybe the unhappy man would give him some answers while under the influence.

"I'd like to talk to you about him," Clint said. "About Mayor Simon."

"Well, sure, friend," Stewart said. "Come on in."

He turned and went into the house, leaving Clint to enter and close the door. When he got to the livingroom the ex-mayor was already pouring two whiskies.

"Drink?" he asked. "Or will I have to drink both?"

"I'll take it," Clint said, accepting the glass.

The room was neat and clean, unlike the man who lived there, who smelled like he hadn't bathed since he lost the election.

"Have a seat," Stewart said, "My housekeeper has managed to keep this place livable."

"She does a great job."

"Yeah," Stewart said, "but doin' a great job ain't always what it takes—what can I do for you?"

Clint sat across from the mayor.

"Mayor—"

"Don't call me that."

"Mr. Stewart," Clint said, "my name's Clint Adams."

"Clint Adams," the drunk man said, squinting. "That name sounds familiar."

"Well, word's been going around that I'm in town."

"The word doesn't get this far," Stewart said. "That's why I don't leave here. Wait a minute, I know who you are. The Gunsmith, right?"

"That's right."

"Somebody send you here to kill Tom Simon? If they didn't, maybe you'll do it for me."

"Why would somebody want to kill him?" Clint asked.

"This town would be better off with him dead," Stewart said.

"And with you back in office?"

"You're damn right!"

"So what's wrong with him?"

Stewart leaned forward in his chair, almost spilling his drink.

"He's a fast talker."

"Aren't all politicians?"

"Not like him," Stewart said. "He doesn't mean a word of what he says. Not one word. There's a germ of truth in what most politicians say, but not this fella, no siree."

"Then why was he elected?"

"Because," Stewart said, "they all fell for it. They swallowed it hook, line and sinker." The older man started to cackle, and then cough. When he stopped coughing he took a stiff drink.

"Mr. Stewart," Clint said, "you don't know what his real plans are?"

"No, sir, I don't," Stewart said, "but whatever they are, they're for his own good, and no one else's. Of that I can guarantee you."

"I see."

"Of course," Stewart said, "if you happen to kill him—"

Clint stood.

"Thanks for talking to me, Mr. Stewart," he said. "I'll see myself out."

Chapter Sixteen

Talking to the old mayor about the new mayor hadn't revealed much.

When he went back to the Queen's Palace Saloon the bartender, Cupp, asked, "More beer?"

"More questions," Clint said.

They both leaned their elbows on the bar.

"Go ahead."

"Is the new mayor married?"

"No."

"Does he have a woman?"

"Yes."

"Who is it?"

"She runs a boarding house in town," Cupp said. "Her name's Martha Folsom."

"I met her," Clint said, "when I was checking around for my friend."

"Handsome woman."

"Does the mayor have any friends?"

"He grew up with Brian Berriman and Tony Bacon."

"And what do they do?"

"Brian owns and runs the newspaper, *The Wentworth Watch*," Cupp said. "Tony . . . well, Tony fancies himself pretty good with a gun. Calls himself Bad Tony Bacon."

"Really?"

Cupp nodded.

"And where would I find Bad Tony Bacon?"

"Usually at a table in the Saddle and Spur."

"I was there, talking to the bartender," Clint said.

"Tony was probably there, too."

"Well," Clint said, "I'll have to go back."

"Why?"

"I need to talk to people who know Tom Simon," Clint explained.

"Still lookin' for your friend?"

"I am."

"And you think Mayor Simon has somethin' to do with him bein' . . . missin'?"

"It seems to me Mayor Simon is up to something," Clint said. "Maybe if I find out what it is, I'll find my friend."

"Did you talk to Mayor Stewart?"

"I did," Clint said, "but he doesn't like being called that."

"Was he drunk?"

"Oh, yeah."

"Too bad," Cupp said. "He was a good mayor."

"Then why did he lose the election?"

Cupp shrugged.

"People are just lookin' for a change, I guess."

"Well, it seems like they're going to get it," Clint said, "but if it has anything to do with my friend missing, it's not going to be the change they want."

He turned and left the Palace.

***

He decided to first go to the office of *The Wentworth Watch* and talk to Brian Berriman. When he walked in, his ears were assailed by the noise of the printing press. The man at the press looked at him and turned the machine off. Then he started wiping his hands on a black rag, but left the streaks of black that were on his face. Through the ink, Clint could see that the man was in his late thirties, as Cupp had said.

"Are you Brian Berriman?"

"That's right," Berriman said. "Who are you? What can I do for you?"

"Clint Adams."

Brian looked surprised, then covered it by trying to appear interested.

"Are you here so I can interview you for my paper?" he asked.

"No," Clint said, "no interview."

"Then what can I do for you?"

Clint took a look around. Everything seemed to be in that one room: the printing press, a desk, a typesetter's table and a filing cabinet.

"I'm here to talk to you about the mayor, and a man named Bad Tony Bacon?"

"Are you after Tony?"

"I don't even know Tony."

"But you know his nickname."

"Seems a lot of fellas in this town have flowery nicknames," Clint informed him. "I'm looking for somebody with a nickname, too. His name's Ben Fentington, also known as Potatoes."

"Potatoes Fentington?" Berriman asked. "I don't know anybody by that name."

"But you do know Simon and Bacon, right?"

"Well, yeah," the newspaper editor said, "we grew up together."

"Well then," Clint said, "we have some things to talk about."

Chapter Seventeen

Berriman sat at his desk. There was one other wooden chair in the room and Clint took it.

"Do you want a drink?" Berriman asked. "I've got a bottle of whiskey around here somewhere."

"No thanks," Clint said. "I just want to talk."

"About what?"

"I told you," Clint said. "Simon and Bacon."

"They're just two guys I grew up with."

"No," Clint said, "one is the mayor, and one's a gunman."

"Tony? He's no gunman. He just thinks he is."

"And Tom Simon's the mayor."

"Well, yeah . . ."

"Do you know what he's planning?"

"He promised to make things better for the town," Berriman said.

"And how does he plan to do that?"

"I don't know," Berriman said, "he just talked about making big changes."

"What kind of changes?"

"Well, for one thing," Berriman said, "he wants to change the name of the town."

"Does he want to call it Simonville, or something like that?"

Berriman shrugged. "I just know I'll have to change the name of my paper."

"And you're not happy about that?"

"No."

"So did you vote against changing the town's name?" Clint asked.

"There was no voting."

"Isn't there a town council?"

"Yeah, but I'm not on it. Even if I was, they didn't get to vote."

"The town newspaper editor is usually on the council," Clint pointed out.

"I know," Berriman said, "but not here."

"And no voting?" Clint said. "Everybody went along with that?"

"Tom is very, very good," Berriman said. "He convinced everyone."

"Everyone?" Clint asked.

"Well," Berriman said, "he won the election in a landslide. Almost everyone."

It seemed like Tom Simon was keeping his plans close to his vest, like a good poker player.

"All right," Clint said, "tell me about Bacon. Why is he called Bad Tony?"

"Because when he was a kid," Berriman said, "he was bad."

"That's it?"

"That's it," Berriman said, "other than the fact he likes the way it sounds."

"Has he ever killed anyone?"

Berriman didn't answer right away.

"Mr. Berriman?"

"I'm thinking," Berriman said. "He says he has, of course, but I've never seen him kill anyone."

"Would he talk to me?" Clint asked.

"Definitely," Berriman said. "You're the Gunsmith. He probably thinks he's faster than you."

"I'm hoping not to give him the chance to find out," Clint said. "I just want some information."

"About Mayor Simon?"

"Exactly" Clint said. "Is he closer with the mayor than you are?"

"Like I said, we all grew up together, but I wouldn't say any of us are close."

"But he wouldn't draw his gun as soon as I walk into the Saddle and Spur?"

"I doubt it very much."

"Thanks for your time."

Clint rose and started for the door.

"You know . . ." Berriman said.

He turned.

"If you did kill him it would make a good story for my paper."

"It's up to you what makes a good story for your newspaper, Mr. Berriman."

"But I was just thinking . . ."

"Yes?"

"If he killed you," the editor went on, "it would make a great story."

"Well," Clint responded, "like I said, I'm not looking to have it happen, either way."

"What if he doesn't give you a choice?"

"Most of the men I've killed in my lifetime haven't given me much of a choice."

Berriman watched the Gunsmith walk out onto the street, wondering if the man was walking right into the mouth of whatever Tom Simon was planning.

Chapter Eighteen

Clint went back to the Saddle & Spur Saloon, wondering if Tony Bacon had been inside when he was last there, and if the man was in there now.

He entered and approached the bar. The bartender, Goode, didn't look like his attitude had improved.

"You're back." It wasn't a question.

"I'm back."

"And I suppose you want a clean glass."

"I want Tony Bacon."

"What?"

"Bad Tony Bacon," Clint said. "Which one of these men is he?"

"Whataya want with Tony?"

"Just do me a favor," Clint said, "and point him out."

"You ain't gonna shoot up my place, are ya?" Greg Goode asked.

"And if I did," Clint asked, "and I left broken glass and blood all over the place, who would notice?"

"Whataya mean?"

Clint turned and looked at the room. There were about half-a-dozen men there, sitting at four tables.

"Which one of you gentlemen is Tony Bacon?" he asked.

"Who's askin'?" one man replied.

He was sitting at a table with another man, both of them working on beers. They were both the right age for the man he was looking for.

"Clint Adams."

"What do you want with Tony?" the man asked.

"Just to talk."

The man who was speaking looked at his friend, who nodded.

"This is Tony," he said, pointing to the other man.

"Eddie," Bad Tony Bacon said, "take a walk and make room for the Gunsmith."

"Sure, Tony."

Eddie got up and walked to the bar, then waved his arm, indicating Clint should take his place.

"Thanks," Clint said.

He walked over and sat down across from Tony Bacon, who was wearing a gun on his right hip.

"You wanna beer?" Tony asked.

"Not here," Clint said.

Tony laughed.

"Can't blame you for that," he said. "What can I do for you?"

"I heard from Brian Berriman that you, he and the mayor grew up together."

"What about it?"

"I'm interested in Tom Simon."

"Why?"

"Apparently, he has some big plans for this town," Clint said. "I'm wondering what they are."

"Again, why?"

"I'm wondering if it has something to do with a friend of mine, who's missing."

"Whataya mean, he's missin'?"

"He asked me to meet him here, and I can't find him."

"What's his name?"

"Ben Fentington," Clint said. "His friends call him Potatoes."

"That's a stupid name."

"You mean," Clint asked, "unlike 'Bad' Tony Bacon?"

Bacon's face turned red.

"You know," he said, "if you have questions about the mayor, maybe you should be askin' the mayor."

"You're probably right, Tony," Clint said. "I just thought I'd take the opportunity to meet you."

"What for?"

"Folks in town say you're fast with a gun."

"So?"

"So I'm going to be here for a few more days, at least," Clint said. "I just don't want you getting any ideas."

"Are you worried, Mr. Gunsmith?" Tony Bacon asked, with a smirk.

"I am," Clint said, "but not about myself."

Bacon's face darkened, this time, feeling he was being insulted.

"Like I said," he finally said, "if you got questions about the mayor, then go ask him. I ain't talkin' to you no more."

"Just remember what I said," Clint responded, standing up. "Guns aren't a game."

"You think I don't know that?" Bacon snapped. "I've shot people, and I been shot at."

"Have you ever been shot?"

That stopped Bacon for a moment, then he said, "No."

"Has anyone here ever seen you kill someone?" Clint asked. "Anybody in this town?"

"Well, sure . . ."

"Don't be telling stories, Tony," Clint said. "You could end up having people look for you who actually know what they're doing."

"Like you?"

Clint didn't answer. Instead, he turned and left.

Chapter Nineteen

The next step was to talk to Mayor Tom Simon, but Clint decided to leave that for the next day. And then he remembered Martha Folsom. Her boarding house was on the way back to his hotel, so he stopped by and knocked on the door.

The woman who answered wasn't Martha Folsom, but an older woman wearing an apron.

"We're not takin' in any more boarders right now," she said.

"I'm not looking for a room."

"Oh," the woman said, "I'm sorry. So what are you lookin' for?"

"Mrs. Folsom?" Clint said. "Or is it Miss."

"It's Mrs.," the woman said. "She's a widow."

"And you?"

"I'm Henrietta," she said, "the cook."

"Ah," Clint said, "well, something smells good, sorry I interrupted you. Is she home?"

"I'm afraid not," Henrietta said. "She's having supper out, tonight."

"With the mayor?"

The woman looked surprised.

"So you know about that?"

"Do people not know about it?" he asked.

"Well," she said, "the opinion in this house is that it's not general knowledge."

"Maybe so," Clint said, "but I happened to hear about it."

"In that case, yes, she's with the mayor."

"In a restaurant?"

"In his home," she said, sniffing.

"You don't approve?"

"I don't like that man at all," she said, "and . . . well . . ."

"Go on, please."

"Mrs. Folsom is . . . a little older than he is," she said. "What's he doin' with her?"

"Some men like older women," Clint said. "And as far as I could see, she's quite attractive."

"You are definitely more in her age range than he is," she commented.

"Is that the only reason you don't like him?"

"No," she said, "I voted for Mayor Stewart. I just didn't like the things Tom Simon was sayin'."

"Well, thanks for talking to me, Henrietta."

"Should I tell Mrs. Folsom you were here askin' for her?"

Clint hesitated then said, "Oh, why not? I'll come back during the day."

"I'll give her the message, sir."

She backed up and closed the door in his face, cutting him off from the good smells. He found himself wishing she had invited him in to eat.

***

Heading back to his hotel, Clint came across a small café that had some interesting aromas of its own wafting out the door. He decided to stop and try it out.

Inside he saw about a dozen tables, half of which were occupied.

"Table, sir?" a middle-aged waiter asked.

"Yes," Clint said, "in the back, away from the windows and door."

"Of course, sir. This way."

Clint sat at his table and asked, "What is that I smell?"

"A combination of things, sir," the waiter said. "My wife is making some beef stew, as well as frying some steaks and pork."

"I'll try the beef stew, then."

"Good choice," the waiter complimented him. "She's also just made a fresh batch of bread."

"Sounds good. Top it all off with a beer, and I'll be a happy man."

"Comin' up!"

It took about ten minutes to get Clint set up with everything he wanted. He noticed the people around him were taking great pains to ignore him, but it suited him tonight. He concentrated on his meal and they did the same.

***

He thanked the waiter, paid for his meal and headed back to his hotel. Why would people be pointedly ignoring him unless they had been told to? Perhaps someone thought too much attention would drive him out of town. And, for some reason, they didn't want him to go.

What could the reason be?

What did it have to do with Mayor Tom Simon's plan to make the town better?

And was Ben Fentington involved, at all?

These were the questions he was going to have to put to the mayor, himself.

Chapter Twenty

Clint decided his meeting with the mayor should take place right in the man's office, so after breakfast he headed right to City Hall.

As he entered the mayor's outer office, a young man looked at him and raised his eyebrows.

"Can I help you?"

"What's your name?"

"Rick Croxton," the young man said. "Who are you?"

"You know who I am."

The man didn't bother to deny it.

"The Gunsmith."

"Right the first time," Clint said. "Tell the mayor I'd like to talk to him."

Croxton stood up.

"In fact, forget that. Just take me in there."

"I can't just—"

"Yeah," Clint said, "you can."

Croxton studied Clint for a moment, looked at his gun, then said. "Follow me."

He led the way to the door of the mayor's office, opened it and marched in.

"Rick," Simon said, "what the hell—we talked about knocking—"

"Clint Adams is here, Mr. Mayor," Croxton said, cutting him off.

Clint walked in behind Croxton.

"All right, Rick," Simon said, remaining seated behind his desk. "That's all."

"But Mayor—"

"We'll be fine," Simon said. "Go! And close the door."

Croxton backed out the door, closing it behind him.

"Mr. Adams," Mayor Simon said, "I heard you were in town."

"Apparently, everybody's heard I'm in town. You care to tell me how?"

"How would I know that?" Simon asked. Clint noticed he was wearing an expensive black suit that made him look more like a gambler than a politician. Maybe that had been part of his plan to get elected—which worked.

"People in this town tell me you know everything," Clint said. "And that you have big plans. Or, at least, you did while you were running for office."

"And I still do, I assure you."

"Can you tell me what some of those plans are?" Clint asked.

"Why?" Simons asked. "Are you moving here?"

"No," Clint said, "but a friend of mine sent me a telegram from here. He said he was in trouble and needed help."

"And who might that friend be?"

"His name is Ben Fentington."

"Fentington," Simon repeated. "Never heard of him."

"Also called Potatoes."

The mayor laughed.

"The poor man," he said. "So, will you be staying in town long?"

"Until I locate Ben, or find out what happened to him."

"I see. Have you talked to our local lawman?"

"I had a conversation with the marshal," Clint said. "He also never heard of him."

"I'm sorry we can't be more helpful, Mr. Adams," Simon said.

"I'm not convinced you can't be, Mr. Mayor," Clint said. "I just don't know how, yet."

"Well," Simon replied, "let me know when you figure it out."

"Oh, I will, Mayor," Clint said. "You can count on that. Thanks for your time."

In the outer office Clint stopped by Rick Croxton's desk, startling the young man.

"Was there something else?"

"Do you like working for the mayor?"

"It's a job," Croxton said.

"Are you interested in politics?"

"No."

"Tell me, have you ever heard of Ben Fentington?"

"No, never."

Clint decided to forgo the question about "Potatoes."

"Do you have any idea what your boss's big plans are for this town?"

"None at all," Croxton said. "He doesn't confide in me. I have work to do, Mr. Adams. Is there something you need?"

"Yes," Clint said, "I need a list of the members of the town council."

"Did the mayor say—"

"He did," Clint lied. "That's why I stopped here."

Croxton took out a pencil and a piece of paper, wrote down the names and handed it over. Next to them he wrote where Clint could find each one.

"There are ten names here," Clint said. "Who are the ones with the most influence?"

"The top four."

"You're very efficient," Clint said, pocketing the list. "Thank you."

"You're welcome."

Chapter Twenty-One

All he could do was keep asking questions until he got the right answers.

He took out the list Croxton had given him, studied the first four names:

Kevin Hove, owner of the general store;

Jim Murphy, the hardware store;

Graham Andrews, owner of the Queen's Palace;

Libby Jefferies, owner of the Lucky Seven.

These were the four people he was going to talk to first. If he got what he wanted from them, he wouldn't need to talk with the other six on the list.

First, Kevin Hove . . .

***

He approached the general store as a family was coming out—a father, mother, and two small children, a boy and a girl. When she saw him the mother immediately put her arms around her children's shoulders and hurried them away. The father rushed after them.

He entered the store, saw there were several other customers. Only one person was working there, a man in his forties, standing behind the counter. Clint waited until he had served all of the customers, and the store was empty. He didn't know how long he would have before more customers came in.

"Can I help you?" the man asked.

"Are you Kevin Hove?"

"That's right," Hove said. "And you're Clint Adams."

"How do you know that?"

"Because I know everyone in town and right now you're the only stranger here. What can I do for you?"

"I understand you're an influential member of the town council," Clint said.

"That depends on who you're talking to," Hove said.

"Rick Croxton."

Hove looked surprised.

"That surprises you?"

"I wouldn't think Rick had that high of an opinion of me—or anyone, for that matter."

"He also told me that Jim Murphy, Graham Andrews and Libby Jefferies were influential."

"We all used to be," Hove said, "when the town and the council were run by Mayor Stewart."

"Mayor Simon doesn't rely on you as much?"

Hove laughed shortly. Almost like a bark.

"Tom Simon doesn't rely on anyone but himself."

"I understand he's got big plans for this town."

"So he says."

"He hasn't filled you in?"

"He's not telling anyone anything," Hove said. "He's keepin' it all to himself."

"There must be someone he confides in," Clint said. "A woman?"

"Simon? With a woman?"

Clint wondered if Hove was aware of the mayor's relationship with Martha Folsom, and not letting on?

"Believe me," Hove said, "Tom Simon's got no time for anybody but himself."

"What do you think he's planning?"

Hove studied Clint for a moment.

"Why are you interested?"

"Because a friend of mine is missing," Clint said. "I was supposed to meet him here, and I can't find him."

"What's his name?"

"Ben Fentington."

"I never heard of him."

"Yeah," Clint said, "that's what everybody says."

"And you think we're all lying?"

"I think somebody's lying," Clint said, "and I intend to find out who."

"Well, not from me."

"Because you won't tell me?"

"Because I can't," Hove said, "because I don't know."

"Well, maybe one of your town council colleagues does."

"Good luck with that," Hove said.

"I'm not done asking questions, Mr. Hove," Clint said. "You can bet on that."

"Have you tried asking Tom Simon himself?"

"I have," Clint said, "and he was no help."

"Well then, I don't know what to tell you."

"Somebody does," Clint said. "Somebody in this town knows what to tell me, and I'm going to find out who that somebody is."

Hove wet his lips, as if he was going to say something, but then he thought better of it.

"Thanks for your time," Clint said, as another customer entered the store.

"Sorry that's all I had to give you."

Clint doubted very much that Kevin Hove's apology was sincere.

Chapter Twenty-Two

Next, he went to the hardware store to talk with Jim Murphy. Unlike Hove's store, when he entered there were no customers. The man behind the counter was staring at some papers, looked up as Clint entered.

"Help ya?" he asked. Like Hove, he looked to be in his forties.

"My name's Clint Adams."

The man stood up straight.

"You're Jim Murphy?"

"Uh, yeah, that's right," the man said, nervously. "W-whataya want?"

"Just to talk," Clint said, "ask some questions." He used the same line he'd used on Hove, about Murphy being an influential member of the council.

"Somebody's been feedin' you the wrong information," Murphy said. "I sit on the council, but that's about it. "I got no power there."

"Why not?"

"Because the mayor's got all the power," Murphy said.

"And that's okay with the rest of you?"

Murphy shrugged.

"He's the mayor."

"And he's got plans, right?"

"That's right," Murphy said. "Big plans that he ain't told us anythin' about."

"And again," Clint said, "that's all right with the rest of you?"

"Look, Mister," Murphy said, "whataya want from me?"

"I suppose you never heard of a man named Fenting-ton?"

"Who?"

"That's what I thought," Clint said.

"I can't help ya with nothin'," Murphy said. "So if you're gonna kill me—"

"I'm not here to kill anyone, Murphy," Clint said. "But somebody's going to tell me something."

"I—I don't know nothin'."

"Yeah," Clint said, "yeah, I know."

He turned and stormed out.

He needed a new approach for when he spoke to the two saloon owners: Graham Andrews and Libby Jefferies. He decided to stop in at the Queen's Palace and see if Scott Cupp could fill him in.

***

"You want me to tell you about my boss?" Cupp asked.

"No secrets," Clint assured him. "I'm not asking you to betray a trust, or anything. I just need to know what kind of man he is. And maybe you could tell me a little about Libby Jefferies."

"Miss Libby?" Cupp said. "Why do you wanna know about her?"

"She and your boss are on the town council, right?"

"Well, yeah."

"They must know something about what the mayor is planning."

"You'd have to ask them that."

"What's Miss Libby like?"

"Pretty thing," Cupp said, "leastways, she was when she was younger. She's still good-lookin' now, though."

"Married?"

"No."

"I was in the Lucky Seven," Clint said. "It's not the best place in town, but it's not the worst."

"No," Cupp said, "the worst is the Saddle and Spur."

"Right," Clint said. "Been there, too."

"Well, it's popular," Cupp said, "but usually when she's there."

"Does she . . . perform?"

"No," Cupp said, "she's just . . . there. People—men—like bein' around her."

"She wasn't there when I went in," Clint said. "I'll have to go back."

"Go back there late at night," Cupp said. "Except for meetings of the town council, she hardly ever comes out during the day."

"I'll do that, thanks," Clint said. "Now what about your boss?"

"He stays in his room, or his office," Cupp said. "He don't mix with the customers."

"Another night owl."

"No, that ain't it, at all," Cupp said. "He's usually up early and in his office, doin' business. And he goes out on the street during the day. He just ain't friendly with the customers."

"Isn't being friendly one of the ways of attracting customers?" Clint asked.

"My boss thinks that's the bartender's job," Cupp said, with a grin.

"Well, then," Clint said, "tell your boss for me, you do a great job."

"Hey, thanks."

"Or, I've got an even better idea," Clint said. "I'll tell him."

Chapter Twenty-Three

"Is he in his office now?" Clint asked.

"He should be," Cupp said. "I can go check, but . . ."

"But what?"

"I gotta tell ya, the boss is a good man," Cupp said. "Whatever the mayor's planning, if it's hinky, the boss ain't really gonna be in on it."

"I'll keep that in mind, Scott," Clint promised.

"I mean . . . you ain't gonna kill 'im, or anythin', are ya?"

"Why do people think I'm here to kill somebody?" Clint asked. "I just want to talk with him."

"Sorry," Cupp said, "it's just your reputation, and all . . . I'll go see if he's there."

"Fine," Clint said. "I'll just stand here and finish my beer."

Cupp came from behind the bar and walked to the back of the saloon. Clint watched him knock and go through a door. Within minutes, he came out and walked back.

"He says come ahead," Cupp said.

"Thanks," Clint said, grabbing his half full mug. "I'll take this with me."

"He told me to give you a fresh one."

"Fine with me," Clint said, and waited while Cupp drew it. "Thanks." He grabbed it and carried it to the back of the room with him.

Clint knocked and entered. He was shocked by the interior. It was a huge room, unlike most of the small saloon offices he had seen in the past. Most owners used the space for their customers, not for themselves. It seemed like Graham Andrews liked a lot of personal space.

The desk was at the far end of the room, and was itself pretty large. Clint suspected the man himself might be oversized, but as Andrews stood he saw that he was wrong. Tall, and slender, but certainly not imposing.

"Clint Adams!" Graham Andrews said in a booming voice. "Damn glad to meet you."

He came around the desk with his hand extended. Clint was holding his beer glass in his left hand to keep the right free. He shook hands quickly.

"Have a seat," Andrews said, hurrying back around his desk. "Scott tells me you've been drinking in here quite a bit since you arrived in town. Tell me what I can do for you."

"Talk to me about Mayor Simon," Clint said. "I'm trying to figure him out."

"What is there to figure?" Andrews asked, spreading his hands. "He's a politician."

"Which means he's a liar."

Andrews laughed.

"I see we have the same opinions of politicians," he said.

"So tell me," Clint said, "why are you going along with his plans for the town?"

"We need something to bring this place to life," Andrews said. "He seems to think he has the answer."

"But he's not telling anyone."

"You're a gambler, Adams," Andrews said. "You know about playing your cards close to the vest. That's what he's doing."

"So when does he show his hand?"

"When he's ready, I guess," Andrews said, with a shrug.

"And the entire town council is okay with that," Clint said.

"Not the entire council," Andrews said, "but enough of us. Look, Roger Stewart was the mayor here for a long time. Things were starting to go stale. We needed some new blood. Tom Simon is the only one who stepped up."

"Why didn't you step up and run?" Clint wondered.

"Me?" Andrews laughed again. "I'm no politician, and I don't want to be."

Clint found that the man not only had some personality, but charm, as well. He wondered why Andrews chose not to mix with his customers.

"Is that because you'd have to glad hand people, and you don't like doing that?"

"I'd have to smile and lie," Andrews said, "and I don't like doing that."

"Scott says you leave mixing with the customers up to him," Clint said. "He does a great job, by the way, but why don't you like people?"

Andrews hesitated a moment, then said, "Because you can't be honest with them. If I was honest all the time, people would hate me. And if I lied all the time, I'd hate myself."

"I've got to say," Clint responded, "that makes a lot of sense to me."

"In fact," Andrews said, "I'd like you to leave right now."

"You're kicking me out of your office?" Clint asked.

"No," Andrews said, "I'd like you to leave town."

"Why's that?"

"I think if you stay any longer, I'm going to end up having to lie to you," Andrews said.

"And then you'll hate yourself."

"Exactly."

"Then why not just tell me the truth?"

Andrews stared down at his desk for a few moments, then looked at Clint and said, "If you stay, it may even come to that."

Chapter Twenty-Four

Clint gave Scott Cupp a wave on the way out. The bartender seemed puzzled, but if he wanted a report, he could get it from his boss.

Next on his list were two women. Cupp's advice about Libby Jefferies was to see her late at night, so that left the boarding house owner, Martha Folsom.

He walked to it and knocked on the door, wondering which woman would answer, Folsom or Henrietta?

It was a man, eating an apple. He was in his twenties, dressed in trail clothes, although they hadn't seemed to have spent much time on the trail.

"Help ya?"

"I'm looking for Martha Folsom."

"Come on in," the man said. "I'll get 'er. Who should I tell 'er you are?"

"Clint Adams."

"Adams?" He stopped short, took a look at Clint then said, "I'll get 'er," in an entirely different tone of voice. "Come on, in, come on, in."

Clint stepped inside, closed the door behind him. He stood in a hallway and decided to just wait there for Folsom to come and get him.

When she came she was alone, wearing a long blue dress that extended down to her ankles and up to her neck.

"Mr. Adams," she said. "Henrietta told me you were looking for me. Come in. Would you like something to drink?"

"No, no, I'm fine," Clint said.

"Come with me, then."

She turned, started away, and he followed. They passed a doorway where he saw a room with furniture, and a few people lounging.

"That's the sitting room for my boarders," she said. "My office is over here."

She led him to another doorway. "Right in here."

It was a small room, with only a chair and desk.

"It's not much," she said, "but I pay my bills here, and get some alone time." She closed the door, then turned to face him. "What can I do for you?" She settled a hip on her desk top.

He decided to play it straight with her and see where that got him.

"I've been in town looking for a friend of mine who sent me a telegram," he said. "He told me to meet him here, but now I can't find any sign that he was ever here."

"What's his name?"

"Fentington, Ben Fentington."

"No," she said, frowning, "no one by that name ever stayed here."

"I think he might have something to do with the plans the mayor has for your town."

"What makes you say that?"

"It seemed to me when I arrived that the people in town knew I was coming," Clint said. "The streets were empty. Later, when they did come around, they were making sure they didn't look at me, like they'd been told to ignore me."

"And you think it was Mayor Simon who told them that?" she asked.

"Who else?" he replied. "He's the one with the big plans."

"Yes," she said, "plans to make this town better."

"That's what he says to everybody," Clint said. "He must tell you more."

"Why do you say that?" she asked, her eyes sliding away from his.

"Because you and he are . . . involved."

"How do you know that?"

"I've been asking questions," Clint said. "You both might think nobody knows, but you're wrong."

She stood up straight.

"Who knows about us?"

"Who do you think?" he asked. "Bartenders."

"Jesus . . ."

"What's the problem?" Clint asked. "Why does it have to be such a secret?"

"I don't know," she said. "It's-it's Tom who wants to keep it secret, not me."

"Well," he said, "I won't tell anyone else."

"I'd appreciate that," she said. "Maybe we just need to be more careful."

"Martha—can I call you Martha?"

"Of course."

"Martha, who *would* know what Simon's plans are?" he asked. "Who's close to him?"

"Nobody," she said. "As far as I know, there's nobody closer to him than me."

"There's got to be," Clint said. "Everyone has close friends."

"Do you?"

"I have a few."

"And do they know all your secrets?"

He hesitated, then said, "No, I suppose not."

Chapter Twenty-Five

Clint left the rooming house after thanking Martha Folsom for her time.

"I hope you find your friend," she said, at the door, "and whatever it is you're looking for."

"I hope so, too."

"You understand I'll be telling Tom about our conversation?" she added.

"Yes, I understand," Clint assured her.

As he walked back toward his hotel he knew he had hours before going to see Libby Jefferies at the Lucky Seven Saloon. He thought about spending more time in the Queen's Palace, but in the end he decided to just go back to his hotel room.

**

Tom Simon was looking out his office window when his door opened. He saw the reflection and turned to look at Martha Folsom.

"What are you doing here?" he asked. "You're never supposed to come here."

"They know, Tom," she said, closing the door. "People know."

"Who knows? About what? Us?"

"Yes, us," she said. "What do you think I'm talking about?"

"How do you know?"

"Clint Adams came to see me today," she explained. "He knows."

"How?"

"He said the bartenders in town told him."

"Bartenders? Jesus, that means everybody knows. Bartenders can't keep their mouths shut."

"I don't think the whole town knows," Martha said, "but some people do."

"We can't have that," Simon said. "We're going to have to take some time off, Martha."

"But why?" She walked up to him, put her hand on his arm. "We're in love. What's so bad about that?"

"Look," he said, taking her by the shoulders, "it'll just be for a while. Until after."

"After what, Tom?"

"You know what," Simon said. "After I've accomplished what I'm after."

"But Tom—"

"You have to go, Martha," he said, pushing her away.

"But . . . for how long?" she asked, with tears in her eyes.

"I'll let you know," Simon said. "Now go. Get out!"

She turned and ran from the office.

***

Outside, Rick Croxton watched as Martha Folsom ran from the mayor's office in tears. He wondered if he should go in and ask what happened, but decided against it. Chances were good Tom Simon would just bite his head off, even fire him. He decided to leave whatever happened between the two lovebirds alone.

***

Tom Simon sat down behind his desk after Martha Folsom left. He didn't need people knowing about his private life. He was going to have to forgo Martha's company—and her money—for a short time. Once he accomplished his goal, he'd welcome both back into his life.

He watched from his window as Martha hurried down the street, still crying. He hoped not too many people saw her rush from City Hall in that condition.

Clint Adams was still around town, asking questions. Maybe it was time for Tony Bacon to take a more active role. Whether he killed Adams, or Adams killed him, it would work.

He walked to the door, opened it and stuck his head out. Croxton looked up from his desk.

"Rick, get me Tony Bacon."

"Here?"

"Here."

***

Clint waited until nine p.m. to go over to the Lucky Seven Saloon, have a cold beer, and take a good look at Libby Jefferies.

When he had his beer he turned and leaned against the bar. In looking around, he spotted the woman he knew had to be her, seated at a table by herself, wearing a royal blue dress and drinking a glass of champagne. She had lots of midnight black hair piled high on her head, showing off a graceful, pale neck. Now Clint knew why men liked to come here and look at her.

He made a quick decision about how to handle the situation, walked over to her table carrying the beer.

"I was wondering what was taking you so long, Mr. Adams," she said. "Have a seat."

"Miss Jefferies—or is it Mrs.?"

"It's Libby," she said. "Or Miss Libby, if you like. I assume you want to talk?"

"That's right."

"Then sit," she said, "and let's talk."

Chapter Twenty-Six

"What's on your mind?" Miss Libby asked.

"Well, at the moment, you are," he said.

"I'm flattered," she said. "Unless I shouldn't be?"

"You're a member of the town council, aren't you?"

"I suppose."

"You suppose?" he asked. "You are or you aren't."

"Well, I am," she said, "but the council doesn't really have much to do with running the town, these days."

"Because of Mayor Tom Simon?"

"You've heard about him, have you?"

"From a lot of people," Clint said. "Seems he has some secret plans for the town."

"Indeed he has," she said. "I wish he'd let the secret out, already. The town could use it."

"Why doesn't the town council simply insist on it?" Clint asked.

"Because he has them all buffaloed," she said. "I'm the only woman on the council. If I had a few more, we might be able to make some noise. But the men are all under Tom Simon's thumb."

"That's the impression I got when I spoke to them."

"Oh? Who exactly have you talked with?"

"Hove, Murphy, Andrews."

"Ah," she said, "Simon's boys."

"Is that who they are?"

"That's what I call them," Miss Libby said. "They buckled under to him pretty quickly."

"I was given to understand they were the most influential members of the board."

"And who told you that?"

"That fella who works for the mayor, Croxton."

"Him!" she huffed. "He does a lot of Simon's dirty work."

"So he's under his thumb, too?"

"It's not the same," she said. "Croxton is Tom Simon's right hand man."

"So maybe he's the one who knows exactly what the mayor's planning?"

"Could be."

"Then maybe I should get Mr. Croxton alone somewhere and have a talk with him."

"I don't understand your concern over this, Mr. Adams," she said. "You don't live here."

"And I never will," he said, "but I'm missing a friend, and I don't know who's involved."

"But you think it's the mayor?"

"He seems to be the only one with any plans," Clint said.

"What would that have to do with your friend?"

"I don't know," he admitted. "That's what I'm trying to find out."

***

Miss Libby ordered another glass of champagne and offered Clint another mug of beer. He accepted. She waved to one of the girls working the floor, who brought the drinks over.

"I'm afraid I haven't told you anything helpful, have I, Mr. Adams?"

"Maybe not," he said, "but it would be helpful if you called me Clint."

"Fine," she said. "And you can call me Libby."

"Everyone in town calls you 'Miss' Libby?"

"My customers, yes," she said, "the men on the town council. Out of respect, I suppose. I'd rather they respected my opinions, but that's never going to happen."

"What is your opinion?"

"About what?"

"About the mayor?"

"He's smart," she said, "smart enough to know how to play everybody in this town in order to get elected."

"So you think he's a phony?"

"I think he's a politician."

"And a good one."

She laughed.

"There's no such thing as a good politician."

"What about Roger Stewart?"

"Mayor Stewart?" she said, smiling. "He was close. He was a good man, but not quite a good politician. He grew . . . complacent, and Tom Simon took advantage of that."

"Do you think you could get Stewart to run again next time, and beat Simon?"

"Maybe," she said, "but that would be years away. By then, Mayor Stewart may drink himself to death."

"So you know about that?"

"You, too?"

"I went to see him," Clint said, "and yes, he was pretty drunk."

"It's too bad," she said. "I tried to talk to him, but it was no use."

"So you stopped trying?"

She hesitated, then said, "I couldn't let Simon find out I was talking to Mayor Stewart."

"Are you afraid of him?"

"I'm afraid of what he might do."

"Libby," Clint said, "why do I get the feeling you know the whole story?"

Chapter Twenty-Seven

She didn't answer right away.

"I think we should go to my room," she said, finally. "We can talk better there."

"Lead the way," he said.

They stood up and he trailed her across the saloon floor to the stairway on the other side of the room. Most of the customers in the place watched them go.

At the top of the stairs they disappeared from the view of the saloon floor and walked down a hall. They passed a few closed doors before she stopped at one, inserted a key and unlocked it. She led the way in.

She turned, saw that Clint had left the door open, and said, "You can close it. At this stage of my life, there's little that can damage my reputation."

The room looked set up to be half bedroom, half office, with a desk off against one wall, and a filing cabinet alongside it, a bed in the center of the room, and a table with a large mirror against the other wall, alongside a chest of drawers.

"I sleep and work in here," she said. "Spend a lot of my days locked in here."

"You don't like daylight?" he asked.

"With my fair skin? I stay away from the sun as much as possible. Plus, I don't need daylight highlighting my age damaged face."

"What are you talking about?" he asked. "You're a beautiful woman."

"For my age," she said, removing her blue earrings.

"I'm not going to ask your age," Clint said, although he guessed her at mid-forties. "I'm just going to say it doesn't matter. A beautiful woman is a beautiful woman."

"You're very sweet," she said. "Please, sit."

She sat on the chair in front of the mirror, but with her back to the looking glass. That left Clint to sit on the edge of the bed. He noticed that unlike most women he had known over the years, she had never checked her reflection in the mirror since they entered the room. Could this woman really not know how lovely she was, no matter what her age?

"Maybe we should stand," he said, moving to her and putting his hands out. She took them and he pulled her to her feet. When he kissed her, she melted against him.

He moved his lips from her mouth to her neck to her smooth shoulders, felt her shudder and sigh as she moved her hands between them. She touched his gunbelt.

"I'll do that," he said, removing the belt. She had a bed with no bedpost, so he moved her chair over from the dressing table closer to the bed, and hung the belt on the back of it.

"You're a careful man."

"I'm a lot more than careful," he said, taking her in his arms again. He slid his hands up her back to the catch on her dress and undid it. At the same time, she undid his trousers, and in quick order they had each other's clothing scattered all over the floor.

Her body was lush with large breasts, hips and thighs. Her butt could have been a monument to how women should look when they're naked, curved and full. He cupped the heavy undersides of her breasts in his hands and thumbed the dark brown nipples to life.

While his hands roamed over her body, she reached between them to grasp his hardening penis. She stroked it lovingly with both hands for a few moments, then continued one-handed while she moved the other to cradle his sack.

They soon grew impatient and gravitated to the bed together, falling atop it without removing the blanket. They were too involved with each other to worry about bed covers.

They wrapped their arms and legs around each other and kissed feverishly. Groaning and moaning into each other's mouth, their ardor grew.

Clint fully enjoyed his time in Miss Libby's bed, and was glad she had no desire to have sex against a wall. She weighed quite a bit more than Fiona, and holding her up against a wall would not have been easy.

He explored her body further, using his fingers and his mouth. He settled down with his face between her legs until she was good and wet, then plunged himself into her. She hung onto him with incredible strength until her pleasure overtook her and she began to beat on the mattress with her fists. When he exploded into her, they both cried out loudly . . .

***

"I wasn't in bed with a woman who doubted herself," Clint said later.

"Oh," she said, "I have no doubt about my performance in bed, Clint. And now I have none about yours, either."

"I guess we both know each other a little better," he said, getting out of bed and grabbing his clothes off the floor.

"Or not at all," she said.

"That's up to you," he said, pulling on his trousers while she reclined on the bed, watching. "Are we friends, now?"

"I'm forty-five years old, Clint," she said, "and I have very few friends."

When he left the room he wasn't sure he knew what her answer was supposed to mean.

Chapter Twenty-Eight

When he got back to his room, he started to wonder if Miss Libby had taken him to her room specifically to have sex with him. She'd said they'd go there to talk more privately, but maybe her point was not to talk at all. He thought she might be worth another conversation at another time.

***

He woke the next morning with the definite feeling that it was Libby Jefferies who was going to tell him what he wanted—needed—to know. He wondered if she would even agree to see him during the day?

He had breakfast in the hotel, then left to see if the Queen's Palace would be open that early. It was, but it was empty except for the bartender, Scott Cupp.

"You're early," Cupp said. "Beer?"

"Coffee, if you've got it."

"I've got it," he said, "good and strong."

He put a steaming mug down in front of Clint just as Graham Andrews came down the stairs.

"Coffee, Scott," he said, approaching the bar.

"Comin' up, boss."

"'mornin', Adams."

"Andrews."

"What brings you in so early?"

"Just looking for a place to hang my hat for a while," Clint said. "Have some coffee."

"Scott makes the best coffee in town," Andrews said, accepting a mug from the bartender.

"Thanks, boss."

"How's your investigation going?" Andrews asked.

"Investigation?"

"Or search," the saloon owner said, "whatever you want to call it."

"Who do you think I'm investigating?" Clint asked, pursuing it further.

"Okay, look," Andrews said, "after we talked yesterday it occurred to me you might be here . . . investigating . . . something."

"Or someone?" Clint asked. "Like who? You? The mayor? Do you think I'm a . . . Pinkerton, or something?"

"It occurred to me," Andrews admitted.

"Well, I'm not," Clint said. "I just came here looking for my friend, and I'm going to keep looking until I find him, or learn what happened to him."

"Okay," Andrews said, holding up a hand, "sorry. It was just a thought I had."

"Forget it."

"Have you talked to anybody besides me who might've helped you?"

"Can't say."

"I get it," Andrews said. "None of my business."

"Unless you have something to tell me," Clint said.

"No," Andrews said, "I've got nothing—except some work to do in my office."

"Go ahead, then," Clint said. "I'll finish my coffee and get out of here."

"You can stay as long as you like," Andrews said. "After all, you're a customer."

"I'm not going to find Ben in here, though."

"No," Andrews said, "I can guarantee you he's not in here."

Andrews took his coffee with him to his office door and went inside.

"You're havin' an effect on him," Cupp said.

"What kind of effect?"

"I ain't never seen him worried before," the bartender said. "He's worried about you."

"He doesn't need to worry about me," Clint said. "I can take care of myself."

"No," Cupp said, "that ain't what I meant. He seems to be worried about what you're gonna do to him. And maybe to this town."

"I think the people here should worry about what Mayor Simon is going to do to this town."

Cupp nodded.

"Could be some of that, too," the barman admitted.

"Look," Clint said, "how well do you know the other bartenders in town?"

"If you mean are we friends, we ain't," Cupp said. "There ain't a bartender's club or nothin'. Why?"

"I was just wondering if you guys talked among yourselves. And maybe you might've heard something."

"Like what?"

"If I knew that," Clint said, "I guess I wouldn't be asking. Thanks for the coffee."

He turned and left.

***

Outside on the boardwalk he looked up and down the street, trying to decide on his next move. The question answered itself as he spotted the marshal walking across the street. He moved to intercept him.

Chapter Twenty-Nine

Marshal Mark Ellis came up short when he saw Clint Adams blocking his path.

"Adams!"

"Marshal," Clint said. "Sorry, didn't mean to scare you."

"You . . . startled me," Ellis said. "You didn't scare me. What can I do for you?"

"I thought maybe I'd buy you a drink."

"It's a little early for that," Ellis said.

"Not for a man like you," Clint said. "Come on, we're walking in the direction of the Lucky Seven. Let's go in."

"Well . . . sure, why not?" the lawman finally agreed.

"There ya go!" Clint said, and fell into step next to the marshal.

***

Tony Bacon looked at the men he had assembled in the Saddle & Spur Saloon.

"Lock that front door!" he told Tim Kitchen.

"Gotcha!" Kitchen said.

In addition to Kitchen, he had three more men there, all around the same age as he was, thirties.

Kitchen came over and sat with the other three men, and they all stared at Bacon, waiting.

"Clint Adams is in town," Bacon said.

"We heard that, already," Kitchen commented.

"Yeah, well," Bacon said, "there's somethin' you don't know."

"What's that?" Kitchen asked.

"We're gonna kill 'im," Bacon said. "That is, I'm gonna kill him."

"Good for you," Kitchen said, speaking for all four men. "What do we get out of it?"

"We all get somethin' out of it," Bacon said. "The town gets somethin' out of it. It's gonna be the place where the Gunsmith met his match."

"You?" Kitchen asked.

"You wanna try me, Tim?"

"Hey," Kitchen said, "if you say you're fast enough, that's good enough for me."

The other three men nodded. None of them were anxious to take on Bad Tony Bacon.

"So what do we do?" Kitchen asked.

"You four are gonna push 'im in my direction," Bacon said. "This is what you're gonna do."

***

That morning, as he arrived at work and saw Rick Croxton at his desk, the mayor said, "Find me Peace Duncan."

Croxton froze a moment, then said, "What do we want with him?"

"I'll tell him when he gets here," Simon replied.

"Um, but he's—"

"I know what Duncan is, Rick," Simon cut him off. "All you've got to do is get him here."

Simon went into his office and Rick Croxton took a deep breath. Tony Bacon claimed to be a fast gun and a killer, but Peace Duncan was the real thing. Croxton was not looking forward to talking to the man, because Duncan scared the hell out of him.

He got up from his desk and headed for the door, figuring to get himself a drink, first.

***

In his office Tom Simon sat behind his desk and knew he was doing the right thing bringing Peace Duncan into play. The more he thought about it, the more convinced he became that "Bad" Tony Bacon would not be able to kill the Gunsmith. That job was going to have to fall to Peace Duncan. The only difference between Bacon and Duncan was that Peace—a man in his forties who had proven notches on his gun—would want to be paid for his services. That was where Martha Folsom's money would have come into play, but now Simon was going to have to use his own. It would be worth it in the end, though.

That is, if his plan finally did come together.

***

Clint and Marshal Ellis entered the Lucky Seven and, as Clint had assumed, Miss Libby was nowhere to be seen. It was still pretty early for a saloon to be doing a brisk business, so there were only a few customers at the bar, and no one seated at any of the tables.

They went up to the bar and Clint asked the marshal, "Beer?"

"Sure."

"Two beers," Clint said to the bartender.

"Comin' up."

The bartender drew two beers and set them down on the bar.

"You Clint Adams?" he asked.

"That's right," Clint said.

"The lady says you drink on the house."

"Well," Clint said, knowing he was referring to Miss Libby, "you tell the lady I said thanks."

The bartender nodded and moved away.

"Well," the marshal said, "whoever paid for this beer, thanks." He took a drink. "Now what's on your mind?"

Chapter Thirty

"There's something going on," Clint said.

The marshal took another drink.

"You been askin' questions for days, and that's what you came up with?"

"I'm not telling you anything you don't already know, Marshal," Clint said.

"Hey, all I know is the mayor has a plan, and we're all waitin' for it."

"And nobody wants to force him into letting you know what it is?"

"He'll tell us when he's ready."

"I can't believe the town is good with that."

"Look," the marshal said, "you don't live here. You ain't seen people move out, the town gets smaller and smaller . . . Tom Simon is gonna change all that." He put the beer down on the bar. "Now I gotta get back to my rounds."

"Sure, go ahead," Clint said. "Do what everybody in this town is doing—just wait."

Marshal Ellis left the saloon and headed back to his office. On the way he passed City Hall and saw Peace Duncan going into the building.

It looked like the town wasn't going to have to wait much longer.

***

"You're not gonna get nothin' outta him," the bartender said. "Him and Tom Simon grew up together."

"Yeah, I knew that," Clint said. "Maybe that's why I thought I might get through to him."

The bartender leaned on the bar. He was in his fifties, with sparse greying black hair and black stubble.

"Some of the people in this town aren't okay with the waitin'," he said, "but most of them are."

"Them? Not you?"

"Hey," the man said, "I'm just a bartender. If this town dies, I'll move on to the next one and get a job."

"What's your name?"

"Jebediah Dixon," the man said. "Just call me Jeb."

"Well, Jeb," Clint said, "thanks for the words, and the beer."

"Come back any time," Jeb said. "Miss Libby thinks a lot of you."

"We'll see."

He didn't mean "we'll see" if I come back, as much as he meant they'd see just how much Miss Libby thought of him.

***

Peace Duncan walked right past Rick Croxton, who made sure to keep his head down. He didn't like looking at the gunman's face because the man had the deadest eyes he had ever seen. He was slender, dark-haired, and Croxton swore his skin was grey. He looked like death walking.

In the mayor's office Tom Simon stood up as Duncan walked in.

"Thanks for coming, Peace."

"Your little friend out there said somethin' about me gettin' paid."

"Have a seat and we can talk about it," Simon said, sitting back down himself.

Duncan sat across from him.

"What's on your mind, Mayor?"

"The Gunsmith."

"What about him?" Duncan asked. "I heard he was in town."

"He is," Simon answered. "And I need for him not to leave town . . . alive."

Duncan looked interested.

"So you want me to kill 'im?"

"I do."

"When? How?"

"I'll tell you when," the mayor said, "and I want it done right out on the street. But first he's going to face Tony Bacon."

Duncan laughed.

"Bad Tony Bacon?" he asked. "The Gunsmith'll shoot him dead."

"That's what I'm thinking," Simon said. "The Gunsmith will kill Bacon and the men he has with him."

"And you wanna wait until that happens before I kill 'im, huh?"

"That's right."

"And then I get a bigger reputation."

"Right," Simon said, "as the man who killed Clint Adams, the Gunsmith . . . in the main street of a town called Deadville."

Duncan frowned.

"Where the hell is Deadville?"

"Right here, Peace." Simon stood up and waved his arm at the window. "Right down there."

"What the hell are you talkin' about?" Duncan asked.

"I'll explain it to you again, Peace," Simon told him. "Slowly."

Chapter Thirty-One

As Clint walked down the street, after leaving the Lucky Seven, he noticed four men across the way who seemed to be pacing him. They were all in their thirties, wearing holstered pistols. They had a look he had seen many times before. He had been hoping to avoid these kinds of situations, but it seemed as if one was in the offing.

He kept walking, not heading anyplace in particular. He wanted to see what they were going to do.

"Well, lookee there," one of them called out. "Is that who I think it is?"

"Sure looks like him," one of the others answered, "but I ain't sure."

"Maybe," the first man said, "we oughtta go on over there and ask 'im."

"Ya think so?" a third man asked.

"Yeah," the fourth said, "let's do it."

Clint wondered if the performance was just for his benefit, or the benefit of the whole town?

The four men started across the street.

"Hey, hey, Mister," one of them called, as they reached his side, "can we talk to you a minute?"

They all stepped up onto the boardwalk, effectively blocking his way.

"What can I do for you fellas?" Clint asked.

"Are you him?" the spokesman asked. "Are you the Gunsmith?"

"That ain't him," one of the others said. "He's too old."

"No, no," the first man said, looking at his partner, "the Gunsmith *is* old. He's been around for years." The man looked at Clint. "Right, old man?"

Clint knew they were trying to goad him into starting a fight, go for his gun. It had been tried before. What he didn't know was if they were doing this on their own, or they had been sent.

"You fellas know what you're doing?" he asked.

"Hey, we're just tryin' to be friendly," the spokesman said.

"You're trying to push me into a fight," Clint said. "Why? Who sent you?"

A couple of the men frowned and exchanged glances, but the spokesman said, "Whataya talkin' about?"

"Somebody wants you to push me into killing you," Clint said.

"You think you could kill all four of us?" the man asked.

"Judging from the condition of those guns you're wearing," Clint said, "only two of you would be able to shoot back at me. I'd kill the four of you with ease—but that's what somebody wants. Can't you see that?"

Three of the men looked down at their guns.

"What's he talkin' about, Tim?" one of them asked.

"Are you Tim?" Clint asked the spokesman.

"That's right, Tim Kitchen."

"You a fast gun, Tim Kitchen?"

For the first time the man looked unsure of himself.

"Well . . . no."

"Then why are you doing this?"

Kitchen now exchanged glances with the other three men, who were still casting unsure glances at their guns.

"Look," Kitchen said, trying again, "we just wanted to know if you were the Gunsmith—"

"You knew who I was from the moment you started following me," Clint said.

"What's wrong with our guns?" one of the other men asked.

"If you don't keep them clean, you can't expect them to work when you need them," Clint said. "It's bad enough I would've killed you anyway, but you're making it even easier by not keeping your guns clean."

"Look—" Kitchen said.

"All right, then," Clint said. "Let's get this over with. Go for your guns."

He took an exaggerated stance, his hand down by his gun, his feet spread, and waited.

"I—I ain't doin' this," one of the men said.

"Me, neither," another said. "You, you tell Bacon to get somebody else."

"Hey," Kitchen snapped, "shut the hell—" But the three men behind him had already walked away—quickly.

"So, just you and me, Tim Kitchen," Clint said. "You ready?"

"Now wait—"

Clint relaxed his stance and folded his arms.

"You better go and tell Tony Bacon he has to do his own dirty work," Clint said.

"Tony's gonna kill me," Kitchen said.

"I tell you what. If he kills you, I'll kill him. You tell him that."

"Really?" Kitchen said. "Gee, thanks, Mr. Adams."

"Do you know why Tony sent you after me?"

"He just said it was to get you going, so you'd be an easy target for him."

"I see," Clint said. "Well, tell him I'm ready for him any time."

"I'll tell 'im," Kitchen said, stepping into the street.

"And tell him to clean his gun!" Clint called after him.

Chapter Thirty-Two

"Do you understand what I want?" the mayor asked Peace Duncan.

"Pretty much," Duncan said. "You want me to kill the Gunsmith."

"Can you do it?" Simon asked. "Can you take him? In front of the whole town?"

Duncan smiled, something Tom Simon had rarely seen the dour, grey man do.

"I wouldn't have it any other way," he said.

***

The four men were sent to test him by Tony Bacon. Who had told Bacon to send them? Clint's best guess was the mayor. Now he had a feeling he knew what the mayor's big plan was, but he decided to come right out and ask someone if he was right. And the someone he chose was Miss Libby.

He'd have to wait, though, until it got dark for her to come out in the open. He could have gone to her door and knocked, but then he would have caught her off guard with his questions, which might cause her to go quiet on him. He decided to wait until she was comfortable.

That left him with the rest of the day to kill. He kept walking with no particular destination in mind when he saw someone approaching him, very determined.

"Mr. Adams," Henrietta, the cook at Martha Folsom's boarding house, asked.

"Miss—"

"Just Henrietta," she said. "Please."

"Henrietta, then," Clint said, "what do we have to talk about?"

"Martha," she said, "and the mayor."

"How about some coffee?" he asked.

***

Henrietta took him to a small café off the main street, and opted for tea over coffee.

Clint got a cup of coffee.

"What's on your mind, Henrietta?"

"The mayor," she said, "has broken Martha's heart. Did you have anything to do with that?"

"How could I have anything to do with it?" he asked.

"Maybe you said something . . . did something . . . for him to send her away."

"Maybe their relationship just came to an end."

"No," she said, "she still loves him. She's miserable, just sitting in her room, crying. I wish somebody would make that man feel what she's feeling." She leaned forward. "Can you do that, Mr. Adams? Can you hurt him?"

"I'm here to find my friend, Henrietta," he said. "If doing that hurts the mayor, so much the better."

"Well, can I pay you to kill him? That's what you do, isn't it? Kill people?"

"No," Clint said, "that's not what I do." He pushed his coffee cup away. The stuff was weak. "I think we're done here."

"Please!" she said, reaching out to grab his hand. "I'm sorry, I didn't mean . . . I'm just so . . ."

"Henrietta," he said, "I know you're upset, but I can't involve myself in what happens between the mayor and Martha. But if whatever I do has an adverse effect on the mayor . . ." He shrugged.

"All right, yes," she said. "I—I suppose that will have to do."

He stood up.

"I'm sorry."

He left her sitting there, staring into her cup of tea.

***

Clint walked down the street, wondering if something he had done was the reason for the mayor breaking it off with Martha Folsom.

He couldn't lose sight of the fact that Ben Fentington had asked him to come there. Or, someone had used Ben's name.

When he got to his hotel he saw several chairs out front and decided to sit in one. Okay, what if someone had used Ben's name to get him there? How would they have known to do that? And why? So they could kill him? That kind of plan would have to be the act of a desperate or crazy man.

Then he came up with an idea and changed direction. He went in search of the telegraph office.

"Good day, sir," the telegraph clerk greeted him. "Help ya?"

"Just one telegram," Clint said. "I can write it out right here."

"As you wish," the clerk said, and gave him a pencil and a flimsy paper to write on.

He wrote a short telegraph to Rick Hartman, in Labyrinth, Texas, asking him if he had heard anything from or about Ben Fentington. If there was anything in the air, Rick Hartman was the man who would hear it.

"There you go," Clint said, pushing the telegram across the counter.

"I'll just tally that up," the clerk said. "Will you pick up the reply?"

"I'm at the International," Clint said. "Just leave it with the desk clerk there."

"Okay."

Clint paid the man and left.

Chapter Thirty-Three

Clint went back to the International Hotel and once again sat in a chair out front. What else was there for him to do? Hopefully a response from Rick would tell him something. Or perhaps another conversation with Miss Libby would get her to reveal something.

Or maybe while he was sitting there, out in the open, somebody would actually try to kill him. At least that way something would happen.

He thought about Tony Bacon. He had sent the four men to harass him. Maybe instead of waiting to see what Bacon was going to do next, he should push the matter.

He got up and headed for the Saddle & Spur Saloon.

***

"He what?" Bacon asked.

"He scared them," Tim Kitchen said. "They ran off."

"And what did you do?"

"Well," Kitchen said, "they left me there alone with the Gunsmith. What was I supposed to do?"

"So you ran, too?" Bacon asked.

"Not exactly," Kitchen said. "He sent me back to you with a message."

Bacon's eyebrows shot up.

"You told him I sent you?"

"One of the other guys said your name."

"Damn it!"

They were sitting at a table in the Saddle & Spur, with a beer in front of each of them. Bacon slammed his hand down on the table, spilling some beer from each mug. Kitchen grabbed his to keep it from tipping over.

"All right," Bacon said, "what's the message?"

"He says if you kill me, he'll kill you. And, oh yeah, you should keep your gun clean."

"What? What does that mean?"

"That's how he scared the others," Kitchen said, "He told them their guns wouldn't fire because they hadn't kept them clean."

"And they believed him?"

"Yeah, they did," Kitchen said, "and he was probably right."

Bacon stopped himself before he looked down at the gun on his hip.

"There's nothing wrong with my gun," he said.

"Look, Tony, I'm sorry—"

"We're done, Tim," Bacon said. "You can go."

"Tony—"

"Get out!"

Kitchen stood, left his beer, and stormed out the batwing doors.

***

Clint looked over the batwing doors, saw Tony Bacon sitting with Tim Kitchen. He assumed Kitchen was delivering his message, so he decided to wait across the street. When he saw Kitchen come rushing out, he crossed back again, and entered the saloon.

***

Tony Bacon watched Kitchen storm out, and was still staring at the doors as they swung in and out, when suddenly Clint Adams walked in.

And then Tony Bacon did look down at his gun to see if it was clean.

***

Clint almost went to the bar first for a beer, but then remembered about the dirty glasses. So instead, he walked directly to Tony Bacon's table.

"Hello, Tony."

"Adams," Bacon said. "You want a beer?"

"Yeah," Clint said, "but not here."

"I don't blame you."

"Mind if I sit?" Clint asked.

"Suit yourself."

Clint sat across from the man, back far enough from the table so that he wouldn't be impeded if he had to go for his gun.

"Your friend Kitchen give you my message?"

"He ain't my friend," Bacon said, "and yeah, he did. Not that I understood it."

Clint smiled.

"If he told you what happened, then you understood it."

"So," Bacon said, "are you here to make me use my clean gun?"

"I'm here to give you a chance."

"To do what?"

"The right thing," Clint said.

"And what would that be?"

"Tell me what the hell is going on," Clint said.

Chapter Thirty-Four

"Whataya mean?"

"You sent those four men to push me into a fight," Clint said. "Maybe you wanted me to kill them. Or, whoever told you to send them after me wanted me to kill them."

"Nobody told me nothin'."

"Look, Bad Tony—"

"Don't call me that."

"I thought you liked it."

"Not comin' from you."

"Okay, Tony," Clint said, "just tell me the mayor put you up to this and we're done."

"What?" Bacon asked. "Why would I tell you that?"

"The mayor didn't put you up to it?"

"I didn't say—hey, nobody put me up to anything. If you had trouble with some varmints, that's your problem."

"Except that they said you sent them."

"Look, Adams," Bacon said, "don't push me. You won't like what happens."

"Oh, I know that," Clint said. "Whether you kill me or I kill you, I won't like it."

"Why don't you get out of here," Bacon suggested.

"Tony," Clint said, "I'm giving you a chance to get out from under this."

"I ain't under anythin'," Bacon said, "and I don't need any chances from you."

Clint stood up.

"Like I said, if you're going to come after me, keep that gun clean."

Clint walked out.

***

He had accomplished nothing.

Okay, he managed to avoid killing four not-so-innocent men, and maybe he had talked Tony Bacon out of coming after him. But other than that, nothing.

As he entered the hotel lobby, the desk clerk called out to him and waved.

"Telegram Mr. Adams."

"Thanks," Clint said, accepting it. He took it to his room before reading it. Rick Hartman said he hadn't heard a thing from or about Ben Fentington in months. "Last sighting was somewhere in Nebraska."

Fentington had been a lawman, a gunman, a farmer, a miner, a mountain man—he had lived a full life, and "Potatoes" was fairly well known by the people Clint knew—but not in this town.

If Hartman hadn't heard anything about him since he was in Nebraska, then something was wrong. But how did Potatoes have a chance to send him a telegram?

He put Rick's telegram in his pocket and went back to the telegraph office.

***

"Back again?" the clerk asked, as he entered the office. "Got another one to send?"

"No," Clint said, "just some questions."

"About what?"

"A telegram that was sent to me, supposedly from this town."

"Well," the clerk said, "that would've come from me."

"What's your name?"

"Walter Herbert."

"Well, Walter, my friend is a large, lumpy looking man who goes by the name Ben Fentington. Does that mean anything to you?"

Walter thought about it, then shook his head.

"No, I don't remember someone like that."

"He's also called Potatoes Fentington."

"Well, whether he's Ben or Potatoes," Walter said, "I think I'd remember a name like Fentington."

Clint thought the young man was right.

"And when was this telegram sent?" Walter asked.

"Weeks ago," Clint said. "It took some time to get to me."

"So maybe your friend came and went?"

"His telegram said there was trouble."

"Well, now," Walter said, "I think I'd remember one like that. Asking for help?"

"Exactly."

"Yeah," Walter said. "I'd remember that."

"So you're saying it wasn't sent from here, then," Clint said.

"I'm sayin'," Walter replied, "that I didn't send it."

"And does anyone else have access to your key?"

"Well, not usually."

"What's that mean?"

"Somebody could come in here when I'm not around and send a telegram."

"Do you know of anyone else in town who can work it?" Clint asked.

"I don't."

"The mayor, maybe?"

"Why would the mayor know how to work a telegraph key?"

"That," Clint said, "is a very good question."

Chapter Thirty-Five

Peace Duncan was a careful man.

His mother argued with his father over the name "Peace." She thought calling him that would make certain that he'd grow up a peaceful man. His father wanted to call him Duke, for no reason other than it sounded good to him.

But while he had not grown up to be a peaceful man, he had grown to be careful.

He wanted to get a look at Clint Adams, but knew enough to realize a man like Adams would always be very aware of his surroundings. So he was going to have to pick his spot very carefully.

He decided to get a haircut.

In the barbershop he could see the street through the window, and since it was down the street from the International Hotel he figured he would catch a glimpse of the Gunsmith at some point. It just happened to occur while he was sitting in the barber's chair, getting the back of his hair trimmed.

"Stop!" he said to the barber.

"What? I ain't done!"

"Just wait," Duncan said.

The Gunsmith had been described to him, but he thought he probably would have picked him out on his own. When you're a killer, you can pretty much pick the other killers out, even in a crowd.

Clint Adams wasn't in a crowd, he was simply walking across the street. But even if people had not been moving out of his way, Duncan would have known him.

"Okay," he told the barber, "finish up."

"Yessir! A shave?"

"Hell, no!"

***

Clint was ready for a beer, so he was headed for the Queen's Palace. Later, he would change over to the Lucky Seven when he thought he'd find Miss Libby available.

"Beer," he told Scott Cupp.

"Time to kill?" the bartender asked, setting it down.

"A few hours," Clint said. "Too bad there aren't any poker games available."

"I could probably scare one up," Cupp offered.

"No, never mind," Clint said. "I'd better not get involved with cards."

"Suit yerself."

Clint did just that. Nursed the beer, cast his eyes over the room, eventually spotted Fiona working a corner. She grabbed a tray of drinks from Cupp, delivered them and then came over to him.

"Somebody told me you need to kill some time," she said.

"I do," Clint said. "You got any ideas?"

"I've got one."

"Lead the way."

***

Upstairs in her room they undressed each other and did their best to kill the time pleasantly. They used all the walls in her room and, finally, the bed.

He settled her down on her back and nestled between her thighs, face first. He remembered briefly as a young man learning how to do this from an older woman, and he was forever grateful to her. Most men didn't know what they were missing when all they wanted to do was rut, squirt and sleep.

He nibbled and licked her to bursting, at which time she drenched his face. Then he drove his hard cock into her wetness and went in search of his own bursting, as she wrapped her long legs around him . . .

***

"And what am I helping you kill time until?" Fiona asked, later. She was lying with her head on his stomach, stroking his cock in an attempt to bring it back to life. At the same time, he stroked the smooth skin of her back and shoulders, both of which were peppered with freckles.

"I have to meet with someone I hope is going to answer all my questions."

"And who would that be?" she asked.

He decided it wasn't a secret.

"Miss Libby."

She propped herself up, looked at him and said, "Oh, her!"

"What's wrong with her?"

"She thinks she's better than every other woman in town because she owns a saloon and sits on the town council," Fiona said.

"Really?" he said. "I didn't get that impression from her."

"Give her time," she said, sitting up. "She looks down her nose at the rest of us."

"The rest of the women in town?"

"Saloon girls."

"Doesn't she employ saloon girls?"

"Those poor dears complain about her most of all," Fiona said. "I better get dressed and go back to work, or I'll have to ask her for a job."

Chapter Thirty-Six

When Clint entered the Lucky Seven he saw Miss Libby sitting at her table, drinking champagne. She saw him as soon as he came through the batwings, lifted her chin, which he took as an invitation to join her. He was surprised, because it wasn't dark yet, and he thought he would have to wait for her.

As he reached her table, so did a little blonde saloon girl.

"Abbe, bring Mr. Adams a beer."

"Yes, Ma'am."

"Have a seat," Miss Libby invited.

He sat across from her.

"I was wondering if you'd come back."

"Maybe I'm not here for the reason you think," Clint commented.

"Oh? Suppose you tell me your reason then."

"Libby, I think I know what's going on," he said. "I'd like you to tell me if I'm right."

"How would I know whether you're right or not, Clint?" she asked.

"Because you're a smart woman."

"We'll see," she said. "Go ahead."

Abbe came back with his beer, set it down and scurried away. Clint noticed the look the girl gave Libby. She feared and disliked the older woman.

"Okay," Clint said, "I think the mayor wants me dead."

"What?"

"I think he wants me to be killed to put your town on the map."

"What, like Tombstone, or something?"

"Exactly."

"That's . . ."

". . . crazy, I know. But people knew I was coming here, stayed off the street because they thought it would happen as soon as I arrived. Obviously, word went out for people to go back to their normal lives, and not to stare at me."

"The word went out?"

"From the mayor. He didn't want me tipped off to what he was planning."

"Are you serious?"

"Dead serious. I've already been harassed by four men trying to push me into a fight. They were sent after me by Tony Bacon."

"I know Tony," she said.

"Yes, Bad Tony," Clint said. "I think your mayor wants him to be the one to kill me."

"All that talk about Tony's gun?" Libby asked. "It's just that, talk. You'll kill him easy."

"Which would also work for the mayor. He wants an event . . . doesn't he?"

"You think I know?"

"I do, yes," Clint said. "I think everybody knows, but that you might be the one to confirm it for me."

"Why?" she asked. "Because we slept together?"

"Like I said," Clint responded, "because you're a smart woman. And you know this is crazy."

"The idea is crazy."

"Exactly."

She leaned forward.

"No, I mean what you're thinking is crazy. If the mayor really wanted you dead, he'd use somebody better than Bad Tony Bacon."

"Who says he's not?" Clint said. "Who says he hasn't got somebody else ready for after I kill Bacon?"

"So you think he wants you to kill Tony, and then he'll send his real man after you?"

"Sounds like a plan to me," Clint said. "If I kill a local, the townspeople will support the idea. Did you know that the mayor wants to change the name of the town?"

"I knew that, yes," she said. "Our newspaper editor is against it, as are some other people, but I think he'll go ahead and do it, anyway."

"After I'm killed," Clint said, "this'll be the town where the Gunsmith died."

She stared at him. He had an idea there was something she wanted to say, she just wasn't ready to say it, yet.

"Now you're wondering how I figured this out," he said. "and if you should confirm it or not."

"It's . . . madness."

"On that we've agreed, already, haven't we?" He stood up, leaving his beer untouched. "When you're ready to tell me something, I'll be ready to listen."

"Clint—"

"Meanwhile," he went on, "I'm going to do my best not to kill Tony Bacon."

"Well, that's good news."

"Not for the mayor," Clint said. "In fact, why don't you tell him I said that. Maybe then he'll send his real gunman after me, and we can get this over with."

She started to protest, but he didn't give her a chance. He just turned and walked out.

Chapter Thirty-Seven

The shot came as a surprise.

It shouldn't have. Clint was always ready to get shot at. It was the life that he led. But this time, he just didn't expect it. Not yet, anyway.

Immediately, people on the street scattered and, in moments, it was deserted. As Clint dove behind a full horse trough, there were two more shots. From the sound, he knew they were fired from two different rifles. Unless this was the new player, Clint could only think of Tim Kitchen and his three friends. Tony Bacon would have come at him head on, and he was fairly sure if the mayor had himself a real gun, the scenario would have been the same. Mayor Simon was not going to want him shot down in the street from ambush.

Or would he?

Clint studied the rooftops and windows across the street for rifle barrels. Seeing none he decided to move and try to draw them out. He stood and it only took a moment. A rifle barrel appeared from one of the rooftops, and two of the windows, all in the same building—the hardware store. Clint remembered that the store was owned by Jim Murphy, who was also on the town council.

He ducked back down behind the trough when the firing started again. From his vantage point he could see the City Hall building a little further down the street. There was a large window on the second floor, behind which he knew was the mayor's office. He wondered if Tom Simon was standing at that window, watching the festivities. Maybe he had heard what happened with Kitchen and the other three men, and he just decided to have Clint ambushed.

Clint felt he had two choices. Make his way to City Hall and confront the mayor, or get his ass across the street to the hardware store. Once inside he could make his way to the second floor, or the roof.

He decided on the hardware store. Once he got the men who were shooting at him, he could drag them into City Hall and deposit them on the mayor's big desk.

Now the question was, how to get across the street without getting shot? The answer came driving down the street at that point. It was a buckboard, probably from a nearby ranch. The driver obviously had no idea what was going on. As he drove by, looking around at the empty street, Clint left his position and used the passing wagon to get across the street. The shooters started firing at him again, hit the buckboard a few times, causing the driver to duck his shoulders and almost leap from his seat. He snapped his reins at the two-horse team to urge them to go faster. Clint made it across the street to the front of the hardware store as the buckboard sped away.

"What's goin' on?" Murphy shouted as he entered.

"Don't tell me you have nothing to do with this," Clint said.

"With what?"

"There are three men shooting at me from your building," Clint said, "two from the second floor, one on the roof. How do I get up there?"

"You can't get to the second floor from here," Murphy said. "There's an outside staircase along the side of the building."

"Can I get to that from here?"

"Well, you could go out that window," Murphy said. "It'll leave you under the stairs."

"And how do I get to the roof?"

"There's a hatch in the ceiling of the second floor."

Clint started for the window, then turned and said, "Murphy, if you had anything to do with this, don't be here when I come back."

Clint headed for the window, opened it and climbed out. As Murphy had said, he was underneath the stairs to the second floor. He came out from under and started up. As he got halfway there the door opened and two men came rushing out. They probably figured since they couldn't get another shot off at him, they better run.

They stopped on the landing above, staring down at him, rifles in their hands. It was two of the three men who had been with Tim Kitchen.

"Jesus!" one of them said.

They both tried to bring their rifles to bear on him, but he drew and fired quickly. They staggered back under the impact of the bullets. The wooden rail behind them gave way with a crack, and then both fell to the ground.

He didn't bother checking on them. They were dead. That left him with the one on the roof. He needed to get him alive, so he could question him.

He went up the stairs the rest of the way and into the building, gun in hand in case the third man had come down from the roof. The room he was in was empty. He saw the hatch in the ceiling, which was open. The man had to still be up there, unless he had jumped down.

He holstered his gun, pulled a chair over and stood on it. He needed both hands free to haul himself up. If the shooter was waiting for him, he'd be a sitting duck. If he called out to him, he'd be warning him. All there was for him to do was go, and hope.

He reached and pulled himself up.

Chapter Thirty-Eight

He scrambled onto the roof quickly, and looked around. There was no one in sight. But then he heard something, a sound from one side of the roof. He ran there and looked over. A man was trying to lower himself from the top of the hardware building to the one story roof next to it. And he still had his rifle in his hand. The other roof was further down than he had thought.

"You can let go of your rifle and grab my hands," Clint said, "or you can fall and break your back."

The man looked up at Clint, who recognized him as one of the three men who had been with Tim Kitchen.

"You'll pull me up?"

"I will."

"And you won't k-kill me?"

"No," Clint said, "but you have to talk to me."

"I-I'll tell you whatever you wanna know," the man said. "Just don't let me fall."

Clint thought the man could have successfully dropped to the other roof without injuring himself, but obviously the man didn't think so.

"Drop the rifle," he said, reaching out, "and grab my hand."

The man studied Clint's face for a few seconds, the fingers of the hand clutching the roof turning red. Finally, he dropped his rifle to the roof below and reached up. Clint grabbed his hand, and the man let go of the roof.

Clint opened his hand and said, "Oops."

The man fell, his eyes going wide. Clint quickly leaped up on the edge of the roof, and dropped down, landing on his feet. The falling man had landed on his back and lay there, gasping for air.

"You just got the wind knocked out of you," Clint said, picking up the fallen rifle, and plucking the man's dirty handgun from his holster. "Take it easy. It'll come back."

Clint stood aside and waited, more than an arm's length away. Finally, the man sat up and started to breathe.

"What's your name?"

"Chester," he said. "Chester Scott."

"Who sent you after me?"

The man looked up at him.

"What happened to Lew and Willy?"

"The other two shooters?" Clint asked. "Oh, they're pretty dead."

"You killed 'em?"

"I sure did. And I'm going to kill you unless you tell me the truth."

"Hey, all I know is Tim said it was time for us to bushwhack you."

"And where's Tim?" Clint asked him. "Why isn't he here with his rifle?"

"He said—he said you'd recognize him right away, but you wouldn't know us."

"Well, he was wrong," Clint said. "I knew you all right away."

"Uh—" Tim said. He stopped short, rubbed his face with his hands.

"What did Tim say?"

The man shrugged.

"He just said we had to kill you for . . . for everybody's good."

"The good of the town?"

The man nodded, jerkily.

"And you and Lew and Willy, you're real good citizens, right?"

"Well—"

"Only you were also going to get paid, weren't you?" Clint asked.

Chester looked pained.

"Well—"

"Yeah," Clint said, "well . . . what's Tony Bacon got to do with all this?"

"Tony?" the man said. "He's—he's Tim's friend."

"You don't know him?"

"Not real well."

"So you don't know that he's the one who sent Tim after me, and told him to bring help?"

"Look," Chester said, "All I know is Tim said we'd get paid if we killed you. That's it."

"And that was enough?" Clint asked. "Enough for you to kill a man?"

Chester shrugged.

"It was a lot of money."

"How much?"

"A hundred dollars."

"A hundred dollars?" Clint asked in disbelief. "That's all it took?"

"Hey," Chester said, "none of us have ever even seen a hundred dollars."

"And now none of you ever will," Clint said. "Come on, we're going to the marshal's office."

Chapter Thirty-Nine

It was dusk when Clint came down the stairs with Chester. They didn't have to go all the way to the marshal's office. He was waiting for them, standing by the bodies of the other two men, Lew and Willy.

"You had to kill 'em?" he asked.

"They left me no choice," Clint said. "You must've heard they were shooting at me on the street?"

"I heard."

"So I saved you this one." He pushed Chester toward the marshal. "He'll tell you about Tim Kitchen."

"What's Kitchen got to do with this?"

"He sent these yahoos after me."

The marshal looked at Chester.

"I got nothin' to say," the man said.

"He was talking on the roof," Clint said. "Maybe if you take him back up there—"

"Don't tell me how to do my job, Adams," the marshal said, cutting him off. "I'll get somebody to move these bodies, then take this man to my office. I'll probably be lookin' for you later for a statement."

"I'll be around."

Marshal Ellis pointed a finger at Clint.

"Don't let me hear you went after Tim Kitchen," he warned.

"Don't worry," Clint said, "it's not Kitchen I want."

"That's what I'm worried about."

***

Clint went to the Saddle & Spur, but Tony Bacon wasn't there. Surprisingly, the bartender, Greg Goode, was working on a glass with a bar rag.

"Where's Tony?" he asked the bartender.

"Beats me," the man said, with a shrug. "He was here earlier, but then he left."

"No idea when he's coming back?"

"No idea *if* he's comin' back."

"Okay, thanks."

Clint started to leave.

"Hey."

"What?" Clint asked, turning back.

Goode held the glass up.

"This glass look clean to you?"

"The glass would be cleaner," Clint said, "if that rag wasn't so dirty."

When he left the bartender was frowning at the rag.

***

Croxton came into the mayor's office. Simon had sent him to find out what all the shooting was about.

"Well?"

"Three cowboys tried to ambush the Gunsmith," Croxton said.

"Did they get him?"

"No," Croxton said. "He killed two of them and turned the third one over to the marshal."

"Shit!" Simon cursed. "Do we know them?"

"No, but apparently they were sent after Adams by Tim Kitchen."

"Kitchen! He's the one—"

Croxton nodded and finished, "—that Tony Bacon was using."

"Damn it!" Simon said. "Get me Bacon, and Peace Duncan."

Croxton swallowed.

"Duncan?" he asked.

"Yes," Simon answered, "I want both of them in my office as soon as possible."

"Yessir!"

Croxton left the office, wondering if he could get Tony Bacon to be the one who fetched Peace Duncan.

***

Clint wondered if Tony Bacon was in hiding. Had he heard that the ambush was not a success? Did he know Clint would come looking for him?

This time when he entered the Lucky Seven, he expected to see Libby because it was getting dark, but Bobby "Muskrat" Streeter hurriedly waved him over, and set a beer down in front of him.

"I got somethin' for ya," Streeter said.

"From Miss Libby?"

"Kinda."

"What do you mean?"

"She said she wanted me to help you."

"And?"

Streeter leaned his elbows on the bar. There was no one else standing around them.

"There's another gun in town."

"Just a gun?"

"A money gun."

"Working for who?"

"Not sure," Streeter said, "but you can guess."

"The mayor?"

Streeter nodded.

"Who is it?"

"Fella named Peace Duncan. Ever heard of him?"

Clint frowned.

"Yes," Clint said, "but only because it's an odd name for a gunman, Peace."

"Sure is. Even weirder when you look at him."

"You've seen him? What's so strange?"

"He looks like death walking," Streeter said. "He's kind of small, thin, and his skin is . . . grey. He looks like he died, and then stood up."

Clint frowned. The description sounded familiar. Had he seen that man around town and not recognized what he was? He usually knew money guns on sight. They looked . . . hungry.

"Okay," Clint said, "thanks, Streeter. I'll keep a look-out for him."

"Right."

The bartender straightened up.

"Miss Libby not coming down tonight?"

"All I know is, she ain't come down, yet."

"Well, when she does," Clint said, "you tell her thanks for me."

"For what?"

"For letting you tell me about Duncan."

"I'll tell 'er."

Clint nodded and left.

Chapter Forty

"I don't want this messed up," Tom Simon said to the two men standing in front of his desk.

"It won't be," Peace Duncan said. "Just leave it to me."

"Yes, well, never mind that," Simon said. "I want the two of you to do it together."

"What?" Tony Bacon asked.

"You want me to babysit?" Duncan asked.

"I don't need a damn babysitter!" Bacon snapped.

"You do if you don't wanna get killed," Duncan said.

"Look, you grey sonofa—"

"Stop it!" Simon shouted, standing. "You're going to do this together, is that clear?"

"I don't want the blame when he gets killed," Duncan said.

"I ain't gonna get killed!" Bacon said.

"Okay, *if* he gets killed . . ." Duncan amended.

"Look," Simon said, "this whole thing is my idea, and if it goes wrong it's nobody's fault but mine."

"Okay, then," Duncan said. "Just tell us what you want us to do."

Tony Bacon stayed quiet and listened.

***

Rick Croxton listened, too, standing just outside the mayor's door. This was the first time he actually heard the mayor tell somebody to go out and kill the Gunsmith. He knew that was the mayor's plan, but this was the first time he actually realized it was going to happen.

When he heard the mayor tell the two gunmen to use the back stairs, he hurriedly sat at his desk and pretended to be busy as they passed by, ignoring him.

***

When Duncan and Bacon got outside City Hall, Bacon grabbed the older man's arm.

"I wanna do it," he said.

"Can you do it?"

"Yeah, I can."

"Then if he kills you," Duncan said, "I'll kill him."

"That's fine with me," Bacon said, "only he ain't gonna kill me."

***

Clint took up a position across the street from the mayor's office. He realized it was dark and after City Hall hours, but there was still a light in Tom Simon's window and he could see shadows moving about the room. He wondered who he would see coming out.

He was there for half-an-hour before the front door opened and Rick Croxton came out. That's when he realized he should have been watching the rear entrance. If a gunman was going to come out of City Hall, he wouldn't use the front door.

He started to leave when he saw the light in the mayor's office go out. Moving back into position, he waited. In minutes the front door opened and Mayor Tom Simon came out. As he started walking down the street, Clint followed.

He thought Simon might go for a drink or a meal, but instead the mayor went directly home. He didn't speak to anyone along the way. As the man went to his front door, Clint moved across the street and watched. Then Simon stopped and turned quickly, and there was a shot. As the mayor went down, Clint started to run across the street.

Somebody had been waiting on the porch for him, and by the time Clint reached the porch, they were gone.

He heard a groan from Simon and bent over him. There was blood all over the front of his shirt. His eyes fluttered.

"Simon!" Clint shouted at him. "Can you hear me? Who was it? Who shot you?"

"Wha—shot?"

"Yes, you've been shot," Clint said. "Tell me who did it."

Simon's eyes fluttered again, then blood trickled from his mouth and his eyes closed.

He was dead.

Chapter Forty-One

"What the hell—" Marshal Mark Ellis said.

"Yeah," Clint said, "I know."

They stood on the porch and looked down at the mayor's body. Clint had gone to fetch the lawman, and luckily when they returned, the body was still there. Clint was concerned the killer might come back and move it.

"And you didn't see who did it?"

"No," Clint said, "somebody was waiting here on the porch for him."

Ellis stared at Clint.

"And you didn't do it?"

Clint stared back and said, "No!" emphatically. "If I did it, I wouldn't have come and got you."

"Yeah, yeah . . ." Ellis said, rubbing the back of his neck. "The problem is, you're the only one with a reason to kill 'im."

"Well," Clint said, "obviously that's wrong."

"Okay, then who do you think did it?"

"Somebody who decided his plan wasn't a good one," Clint said.

"Like a council member?"

"For instance," Clint replied. "Or somebody who didn't like his idea to change the name of the town."

"So they killed him for that?"

Clint was thinking about the editor of the newspaper, who not only didn't want the town's name changed, but didn't want to change the name of his paper. Was that worth killing for?

"Well, now I'm gonna need a statement from you about the man you did kill, and this one, which you say you didn't."

"What did you get out of Chester?"

"Nothin' more than you did," Ellis said. "Tim Kitchen sent him after you."

"He didn't say who's paying Kitchen?"

"Not yet, but I think it was the mayor."

"That's what I think."

"So if the mayor's dead," Ellis said, "what does that mean for you?"

"I guess that depends."

"On what?"

"On whether or not he paid his money guns yet," Clint said.

"You mean they might come after you, anyway?"

Clint shrugged.

"That's all I need," Ellis said. "Why don't you just leave town?"

"They'd only come looking for me. Plus, I'm still looking for my friend."

"Maybe so," Ellis said, "but then I wouldn't have to deal with it."

"What's going to happen when word gets out that the mayor's been killed?" Clint asked.

"My guess is there'll be a meeting of the town council to name a replacement."

"That's what I thought," Clint said. "You think they'll ask the old mayor to come back?"

"That's a possibility," Ellis said. "I don't know of anybody on that council who wants the job."

"How about Miss Libby?"

"Right," Ellis said, derisively, "a lady mayor." He shook his head at the thought.

"Well," Clint said, "I'll leave you to your job."

"Look, do me a favor," Ellis said.

"If I can."

"Stick your head in the Palace and tell them I need four men at the mayor's house, pronto."

"Want me to tell them why?"

"No," Ellis said, "let it be a surprise when they get here."

"You got it."

Clint walked away from the mayor's house, wondering which way things were going to go now?

***

Instead of sticking his head into the Queen's Palace as the marshal asked, Clint went inside, ordered a beer and told the bartender, Scott Cupp, that the marshal needed four men at the mayor's house.

"What's going on?" he asked.

"They'll find out when they get there," Clint told him, "but somebody shot the mayor."

"Killed 'im?" Cupp asked, in surprise.

"Yes."

"Jesus."

Cupp went to the end of the bar, pointed out four men and told them to meet the marshal at the mayor's office.

"Why?" one of them asked.

Cupp looked at Clint and said, "You'll find out when you get there."

The four men left the saloon, and Cupp walked back to stand with Clint. He leaned his elbows on the bar.

"You didn't do it, did ya?"

"No, but I was there, across the street. Somebody was waiting for him on his porch."

"Jesus!" Cupp said, again. "So what's this mean for you?"

"It means," Clint said, "I could use a beer."

Chapter Forty-Two

Clint was working on the beer when Miss Libby came down. She did that jerky thing with her head.

"She wants you," Cupp said.

"I get that," Clint said. "Give me a fresh one to take over with me."

"Mind bringin' her the champagne?"

"Let me have it."

Clint walked over, loaded down with a tray holding his beer, a bottle of champagne, and a glass Cupp had called a "flute."

"Thank you," she said. "I'll pour. It's a science."

He put the tray down, grabbed his beer, and watched her carefully pour her champagne.

"Did Scott give you my message?"

"About the grey gunman? Yeah."

"So? Anything new?" she asked.

"The mayor's dead."

She stopped with her glass halfway to her mouth.

"What? How?"

"Somebody shot him on his porch."

"Jesus." She set her glass down. "That's gonna change things."

"Some things."

"What's it not gonna change?" she asked. "None of us know what his plan was—"

"Yeah, we do," Clint said. "I do, you do . . . we all do."

She stared at him.

"He wanted to turn this into the town where the Gunsmith died," Clint said. "Change the name. Become like Deadwood, or Tombstone. Come on, what was the name going to be?"

She hesitated.

"You can tell me."

"Clint—"

"It's okay, Libby," he said. "Just tell me."

She sipped her champagne first.

"He wanted to call it Deadville."

"Jesus," Clint said. "No imagination."

"He seemed to have a lot of imagination," she said. "Except when it came to names."

"Tell me about the editor of the newspaper here, Brian Berriman."

"What about him?"

"He wasn't in favor of the name change, was he?"

"Brian just didn't want to change the name of The Watch," she said.

"You think he'd kill the mayor to avoid that?"

"No."

"Just like that?"

"Come on, Clint," she said. "Brian's a newspaperman, not a killer."

"Then who on the council decided to take matters into their own hands and get rid of him?"

"Nobody," she said. "Jesus, the council. We're gonna have to meet tomorrow and come up with a new mayor."

"Like Stewart?"

"That's a possibility," she said, pouring some more champagne. "Hell, nobody else is gonna want to step up."

"And what about the plans to kill me and change the name of the town?"

"Clint," she said, "I don't think any of us were going to let him go through with that."

"I think the grey man was going to take care of that," Clint said.

"But that's why I had Scott warn you."

"And what about Tony Bacon?"

"He wouldn't dare," she said. "He's all talk."

"You think so?"

"I've never seen him do anything else."

"I guess we'll find out."

"But why would he, with Tom Simon dead?"

"Because he and the grey man have already been paid," Clint said. "Or because they've decided they want the reputation."

"So Simon's dead and they'll kill you anyway?"

"We're going to find out," he said. "Aren't we?"

"What about the marshal?"

"He's good for cleaning up after," Clint said. "I don't think he's going to be good for much before."

"So you'll go up against them alone?"

"Is there anyone else?"

"Scott's got a shotgun behind the bar."

"No thanks," Clint said. "He's a bartender, not a gunman. I'd be too worried about him getting killed, and I'd probably get killed myself."

"So what are you going to do?"

"I'll find them," he said, "and get it over with. Right after I give the marshal a couple of statements."

"A couple?"

"Oh, that's right," he said, "you don't know . . ." He went on to tell her about the three men who tried to shoot him in the street.

"Christ. So when will you start looking for them?" she asked.

"Tomorrow."

"And tonight?"

He smiled.

"I thought you'd never ask."

Chapter Forty-Three

Clint spent the night with Libby in her room.

For one thing, it was a pleasurable way to spend the time.

For another, he didn't think anyone would come looking for him there. He didn't need somebody trying to bust in on him in his hotel room the night before he intended to finish everything.

He rolled over in bed the next morning, saw her lying on her back, full breasts leaning to either side because of their weight. He leaned over and kissed her on each nipple. She opened her eyes and smiled.

"That'd be a nice way to wake up every morning," she said.

"If that's a proposal of marriage," Clint said, "I'm afraid the answer has to be no."

"Not the marrying kind?"

"Afraid not."

"Well, don't worry," she said, rolling over to face him. "Neither am I." She reached out and stroked his cock. "But I am this kind."

She leaned over and took him into her mouth, sucked him until he was good and hard, then mounted him and took him inside.

As she rode him up and down, he said, "Jesus, I'm this kind too."

***

Later, while he was down between her legs making good and sure she was awake, she gasped, "Oh Jesus, yeah . . . I've got to go and get the council to meet . . . oh Christ, you're good at this . . . we've got to get a new mayor named, and let the town know about Simon . . . Ooooh, right there . . .

She screamed and gushed, wetting him and the sheet beneath her thoroughly . . .

***

While they dressed, she said, "I wonder if Marshal Ellis has already let the cat out of the bag."

"I'll find out," Clint said. "I've got to go and talk to him, anyway."

"And I'll get ahold of Graham Andrews. He and I can call the council together."

"Right."

They went downstairs together, where Scott Cupp was sweeping the floor, and taking chairs down from the tables.

"'mornin'," he said. "Coffee?"

"No time," Clint said.

"Maybe later," Libby said. "I'm going over to the Palace, Scott. After that I should be at City Hall."

"Right."

They left the Lucky Seven together, split up outside.

***

Clint entered the marshal's office, found Ellis behind his desk.

"Where's Chester?" he asked.

"In a cell?"

"He talking yet?"

"No."

"Did you tell him the mayor's dead?"

"I haven't told anybody," Ellis said, "and I swore the four men who carried him to the undertaker to secrecy—and the undertaker."

"You think they'll all keep quiet?"

"Hell no," Ellis said. "At least one of them is gonna talk up a storm—but not until later, in one of the saloons."

"Okay, well, you need my statements," Clint said. "Let's make them short. The two men I killed fired on me, didn't leave me a choice. And whoever killed the mayor was waiting for him on the porch, got away by the time I got there."

"That's it?"

"That's it."

"What are you gonna do now?" Ellis asked.

"Find Tom Simon's money guns and get this over with," Clint said.

"You're gonna kill . . . what? How many more?"

"Maybe two more," Clint said. "Tony Bacon and Peace Duncan."

"Duncan!" Ellis said. "He's involved? He's one scary sonofabitch."

"Well, I'm not going to kill either one of them unless they force me to."

"If you go up against Peace Duncan, he *will* force you," Ellis said. "He's a crazy man. One way or another, one of you dies."

"And what about Bad Tony?"

"He's all talk," Ellis said. "If you kill him, it'll be murder."

"I'll keep that in mind," Clint said.

As Clint walked to the door Ellis said, "Check back in with me and let me know what happens."

"You should get over to City Hall," Clint said. "The council's going to choose a new mayor."

He turned and left.

Chapter Forty-Four

Clint stopped just outside the marshal's office. He was being watched. He felt it. What he didn't like was that he couldn't see the grey man, but he felt him. But if Ellis was right, a man like Peace Duncan wouldn't shoot him from a window or a rooftop.

He stepped into the street and walked, very deliberately, across. He decided breakfast was in order, and stopped at the first restaurant he came to.

***

"Why don't we take him?" Bacon asked. "Why are we just watchin' him?"

"Because we take 'im when we're ready, not when he's ready," Duncan said. "You see him struttin' around like a peacock? He wants us to step out and try him now. He's posin' and preenin' for us."

"You mean, he knows we're watchin' him?"

"He feels us," Duncan said.

"But he don't know for sure?"

"He knows."

"So he's waitin' on us?" Bacon asked.

"That's right."

Bacon puffed up his chest.

"Then why make him wait?" he asked. "I'll step up and take 'im."

Duncan turned away from the window he had been using to watch the street in front of the marshal's office.

"You wanna step up?"

"That's right," Bacon said. "Why wait any longer?"

"I tell you what," Duncan said. "Let's see where he goes. And when he comes out, he's yours."

"Yes!"

Duncan led the way down the stairs and out to the street, where they spotted Clint's back and started off behind him.

***

"Table by the window, sir?" the waiter asked.

"Hell, no," Clint said. "In the back."

The waiter, a portly, bald, middle-aged man, showed him the way.

"Is there a menu?" Clint asked.

"Sure," the man said. "Steak or stew."

"For breakfast?"

"We'll toss in some eggs."

"Potatoes?"

"Sure."

"Steak."

"Comin' up."

"And coffee."

The waiter smiled. He was missing some teeth, and had an earring through one ear. He looked like he had just disembarked from a pirate ship.

"That goes without sayin'."

Clint sat back. He thought he was going to like this little place.

***

"He's eatin'," Bacon said, looking in the window.

"Get away from there," Duncan said. "As long as he doesn't see you, you'll have the advantage."

Bacon turned and looked at him.

"You sayin' I should shoot him in the back?"

"You'd do that if you were smart," Duncan said.

"Is that what you're gonna do?"

"Hell, no," Duncan said. "If I do it, it'll be face-to-face."

"Then that's how I'll do it," Bacon said.

Duncan laughed.

"What's funny?"

"He'd kill you easy," Duncan said. "Fast and easy."

"You think so?"

"I know so," Duncan said. "Come on."

They moved across the street from the restaurant Clint was in.

"Let's do it," Bacon said. "You and me."

"What?"

"You and me, face-to-face," Bacon said. "Whoever survives goes after Adams."

Duncan laughed again.

"You're jokin'."

"Try me."

"Right here?" Duncan asked.

"Well, no," Bacon said. "Adams will hear the shot and come out. No, let's go someplace quiet, where nobody can see us."

"Kid," Duncan said, "you don't know what you're doin'."

"Oh, I think I do," Bacon said. What's the matter? You afraid to try me?"

"I don't wanna kill you, boy," Peace Duncan said, "but I will if you force me to."

Bad Tony Bacon smiled.

"Then consider yourself forced."

Chapter Forty-Five

Clint devoured his steak, eggs and potatoes. It seemed the night with Miss Libby had given him a voracious appetite.

When he came out, he looked up and down the street, then across. For some reason, he didn't feel eyes on him anymore. Where had the grey man and Tony Bacon gotten to? He wanted to put an end to this today. And maybe there was another way to do it.

He headed for City Hall.

***

Miss Libby and Graham Andrews looked at the other seated members of the town council.

"Are you sure about this?" Jim Murphy asked.

"Go over to the undertaker's and take a look," Andrews said. "I went there when Libby gave me the news. He's laid out there."

They all exchanged looks.

"He was gonna change this town," Murphy said.

"Well," Andrews said, "I guess this town will just have to stay the way it is."

"Now wait," Kevin Hove said. "We know what Simon's plan was. Why don't we just see it through?"

"Maybe," Miss Libby said, looming toward the back of the room, "somebody else has something to say about that."

They all turned and looked at Clint Adams, who had just entered the room.

"Gentlemen," Miss Libby said, "meet the Gunsmith."

***

As Clint entered City Hall he saw Rick Croxton standing outside a closed door.

"Is that where they are?" he asked.

"Yup," Croxton said, "they're trying to decide everybody's future."

"And what's your future, Croxton?" Clint asked.

"Whatever it is," Croxton said, "it sure ain't in this town."

"You leaving?"

"As soon as I can get packed," the deceased mayor's assistant said. "Go on in."

Croxton left as Clint opened the door and stepped through.

". . . somebody else has something to say about that."

He saw the seated men turn and look at him.

"Gentlemen," Miss Libby said, "meet the Gunsmith."

"You fellas still trying to decide if you want me dead in your town?" he asked.

"No wait—" Hove said.

"No, you wait," Clint said, moving to the front of the room. "You all knew the mayor's plan was to have me killed and put this town on the map as Deadville. Well, it ain't going to happen."

"We didn't have a choice," Murphy said.

"You all had a choice, and you chose to go along," Clint said, looking at Libby.

"Well," she said, "I for one am ashamed."

"Oh, come off it," Hove said. "You went along with the rest of us."

"She did," Andrews said, "and so did I. But no more. It's over."

"So now what?" Hove asked.

"You need to find yourself a new mayor," Clint said, "and I need to find a couple of money guns. Who knows where Peace Duncan and Tony Bacon are?"

"Who?" Murphy asked.

"I know who Bacon is," Hove said. "Who's this Duncan?"

Clint looked at Libby and Andrews.

"I've heard of Duncan, even seen him, but I don't know him," Andrews said.

"Neither do I," Libby said.

"Well," another voice said, from the back of the room, "I do."

They all looked that way, saw Tony Bacon standing there with a man's body over his shoulder. He dumped it unceremoniously onto the floor. "Gents—and lady—meet Peace Duncan."

Clint walked to the back of the room and looked down at the dead grey man. His description fit, so he had no reason to believe otherwise.

"You killed him?" he asked.

"Fair and square," Bacon said. "He was sure you were gonna kill me. I had to show him he was wrong."

"Son," Clint said, "all you did was prove that he couldn't kill you."

"Well," Bacon said, "he forced me to prove it. And now I'm gonna wait outside to prove it to you."

"Bacon," Andrews said, "it's over. The mayor's dead, and so's his plan."

"Who killed 'im?" Bacon asked.

"We don't know," Andrews said.

"Did you?" Libby asked.

"Hell, no," Bacon said, "I get nothin' by killin' the mayor. But I do get somethin' from killin' the Gunsmith." He looked at Clint. "It don't matter to me that the mayor's dead. I'll be waitin' outside."

He turned and left.

191

Chapter Forty-Six

"What are you going to do?" Libby asked.

Clint looked at her, and the other members of the town council.

"I know you'd like me to get killed," Clint said. "At, least, most of you would."

"Tony must be as fast as he always claimed," Libby said, "if he killed that man." She pointed.

"Does anybody know if this really is Peace Duncan?" Clint asked.

Like I said," Graham Andrews answered. "I don't know him, but I've seen 'im. That's him."

"Word is he was fast," Clint said, "so I guess Tony was faster."

"Could he be faster than you?" Libby asked.

"I guess we're going to find out."

He started out the door, then stopped and looked back.

"I know what most of you are thinking," he said. "You win either way, whether he kills me or I kill him. Well, if he kills me I can't stop you from doing what you want. But if I kill him, I'd advise most of you not to be here when I come back in. But before you leave, decide on your new mayor."

***

Kevin Hove looked at Libby and Andrews.

"Did he mean what I think he meant?" Hove asked. "If we're here when he comes back he'll kill us?"

"Not me," Libby said.

"Not me, either."

Hove, Murphy and a few others exchanged looks, then got up and filed out.

"What about the new mayor?" Libby called.

At the door Hove said, "You and Graham pick 'em. Anybody you want." He went out the door, shouting, "Out the back!"

"You want the job?" Libby asked Andrews.

"Not me! You?"

"Oh, not me," she said.

They stared at each other.

"Roger?" she asked.

"Our old mayor," Andrews said. "Who else? You ask 'im."

"I'm not ready to go out there, yet."

"You don't want to see the shoot out?" he asked.

"Not particularly."

Andrews shrugged and sat down.

"So we'll wait," he said.

***

Clint stepped out of City Hall, saw Bad Tony Bacon waiting for him in the street.

"You really want to do this, Tony?" Clint asked.

"The truth?" Bacon asked. "I wasn't sure I could. But then Duncan pushed me, and I outdrew him clean, Adams. So yeah, I think I'm ready. You see, I think he was faster than you, which makes me faster than both of you."

Clint looked around. The street was deserted, but there were people in some of the windows overlooking the street.

"The word got around fast," he said.

"It does that here," Bacon said.

"Say, what happened to your friend Kitchen?"

"If you think he's on a roof with a rifle, forget it. He left town when you killed the others."

"So it's just you and me, then."

"Just you and me," Bacon said. "That's the only way I make a name, isn't it?"

Clint stepped into the street.

"One way or another," he said.

He stopped.

"You ready?" Bacon asked.

"Whenever you are, Tony."

Tony's whole body was vibrating. He was excited. He was alive in that moment—and dead in the next.

Clint was shocked. The kid was fast—so fast he almost cleared leather before Clint shot him in the chest. The look on Bacon's face was one of sheer surprise. Then his facial muscles went slack, and he fell forward into the dirt.

Clint turned and saw Marshal Ellis watching.

"Another body to clean up," he said.

"Last one, I hope."

"Last one I'm going to be involved with," Clint said, ejecting his spent shell, replacing it with a live one, and holstering his gun. "I'm finished here. Oh, what about my friend Fentington?"

Ellis looked sheepish.

"He was here for a day, just passin' through. Got drunk, bragged he knew you and that you were friends, and then he moved on. But Mayor Simon decided to use his name to draw you here."

"So he's fine?"

Ellis shrugged.

"Unless he got himself killed when he left here."

"Thanks for letting me know."

He started away.

"What about the mayor?" Ellis asked.

"What about him?"

"Who killed him?"

"I don't care."

"Come on, Adams," Ellis said. "You've got to have some idea. Don't just leave me hanging."

Clint walked over to him as people began to come out onto the street now that the shooting was over.

"If I was you," he said, "I'd look for somebody with a motive."

"Like who?"

"Like maybe," Clint replied, "a lovesick woman with a broken heart."

"A broken—aw, you mean—"

"Ask her," Clint said. "I get the feeling that faced with it, she'll confess."

"Aw, Christ!"

He started away, deciding not to go back into City Hall. He would just saddle his horse and be on his way. But then he turned back.

"Oh, and do yourself and the whole town a favor."

"What's that?"

"If you do change the name of the town," he said, "don't make it Deadville. That's terrible!"

Coming May 27, 2019

THE GUNSMITH
447
Boots and Saddles

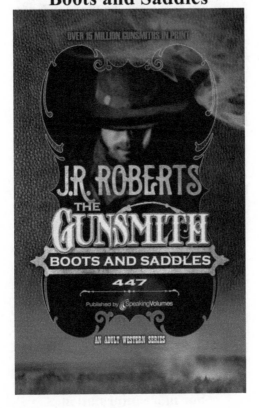

For more information
visit: www.SpeakingVolumes.us

On Sale Now!

THE GUNSMITH
445

For more information
visit: www.SpeakingVolumes.us

On Sale Now!

THE GUNSMITH *series*
Books 430 – 444

For more information
visit: www.SpeakingVolumes.us

Coming Soon!

Lady Gunsmith 7
Roxy Doyle and the James Boys

For more information
visit: www.SpeakingVolumes.us

On Sale Now!

Lady Gunsmith 6
Roxy Doyle and
the Desperate Housewife

On Sale Now!

Lady Gunsmith *series*
Books 1-5

For more information
visit:

On Sale Now!

TRACKER *series*
by Award-Winning Author
Robert J. Randisi (J.R. Roberts)

On Sale Now!

MOUNTAIN JACK PIKE *series*
by Award-Winning Author
Robert J. Randisi (J.R. Roberts)

For more information
visit: www.SpeakingVolumes.us

Sign up for free and bargain books

Join the Speaking Volumes mailing list

Text
ILOVEBOOKS
to 22828 to get started.

Message and data rates may apply.